Moch

M. A. PRICE

Books by M A Price

THE UNFORGIVEN SERIES
The Caged Kingdom
The Heir to Chaos – July 2019
Ivloch – Novella

ISBN Number: 978-1-9160965-1-6

Cover design by Mark Skinner

Edited by: Heather Titus

Published by Thirteen Worlds Press.
First Edition Print.
www.mapricewriting.com

Dedication:
To Brad,
You loved this story and I love you.

Contents

One

Master Reeves was stronger than he looked. It wasn't the first time Ivloch Youchnore had thought such a thing and he doubted it would be the last.

The small man hobbled towards him, his hunched back making the trek slow and hard. The white hair on his head, missing at the crown, flew behind him in the wind. Six moon turns he had worked as Master Reeves' apprentice and steward.

He had grown to love the man, worship him even, but he needed more.

Reeves paused, leant on his cane and rifled in the deep pockets of the cream robe he always wore.

"Well boy, this is yours." He produced an envelope and Ivloch moved to take it from him. "Open it then, boy."

The parchment felt heavy in his large hands, as if the weight of the words it contained rested heavily on him.

"How do you expect to know if you've passed my tests? If you're going to be learning to fight? You claim it's what you want, boy. Well, grow a back bone and have a look then." Reeves snorted and banged his cane on the stone floor. "You want to be my servant forever? Continue emptying my chamber pot? The boy that hides in the shadows. Boy…"

Ivloch listened to the words but tried to let them wash over him. It had become quite the skill he learnt from listening to Ma and could be applied just as easily to Master Reeves, as much as he respected them both. You answer but you don't let the words burn.

He gingerly began to open the letter.

This letter would tell him if his dreams could come true, if Reeves had given him permission to move on to learning with his second, Herman. He had learnt under Reeves previously, when the Master had been in his prime and was the best freelance sellsword in Brodanna. A name feared and reverenced in every hall. Here in Rightwy, of all places, only for the summer and awakening seasons.

One novice he would take on and no more.

Ivloch had begged to be put forward by Master Reeves. He knew his chances were slim; it was such a sought-after position, one that applicants from across the Kingdom had petitioned to be considered for. Rumour suggested that even a Lord from the court in Tonkara had applied.

The parchment in the envelope did not say as much as he hoped. Only one word.

Yes.

Ivloch looked down at the old man. A grin had spread across his weathered face. He was almost blind now, but the senses he still possessed would have told him Ivloch had finally acted on his torrent.

"You've told Herman Croft to train me?" He wanted to jump for joy, but he knew that would mean hitting his head on the low hanging ceiling.

"Yes, but it's always best if you make people think it's their idea. That's a free lesson for you. You're still to work for me directly whenever he is off doing whatever he likes to do. You hear me boy? You'll be hard at work. No time for that manhood of yours to get busy anymore. Train, and me. Train, and me…"

Ivloch felt himself blush. Master Reeves was not prone to remembering boundaries, but he hadn't expected talk of his manhood. The fact that Reeves thought he was doing anything with it at all was quite astounding.

"Every moment I'm not with Herman," he solemnly promised. Reeves shook his head.

"I should hope not boy. Don't want you hanging over my bed, now, do I? A man needs alone time. Stupid boy."

Ivloch tried to supress a chuckle and failed, Reeves could be infuriating at times, but he had got used to his odd ways. He knew that if the Master truly disliked him then he never would have employed him, let alone let the apprenticeship occur.

"Why me?"

"You're big boy, could be useful. Your size will annoy Herman and I do like it when he's irate." He chuckled, but Ivloch wasn't entirely sure he told the whole truth.

"Go on then, boy. Go have a drink with your little friends. Celebrate. Do something that makes my old bones jealous. You're going to have a busy moon tomorrow."

Ivloch decided not to press the issue but allowed himself to give the Master a fleeting hug before he dashed out the door embarrassed.

Two

Ivloch couldn't stop a smile spreading across his wide face as he left Master Reeves' square little house and made his way across the village. Reeves' last words about a drink were playing on his mind.

He couldn't decide if it had been a good idea or not. Little Kreg wouldn't be in The Seven Whiskers yet, Len the Blacksmith would keep him working for another hour. Lusha wouldn't be visiting for another moon turn, his work with the King's Men taking him away. There would be others there. People he recognised but didn't know if talking to was wise.

Men that Ma spoke to that took great delight in presenting their daughters. Some were obvious about it. Drawings of them shoved in his face, 'accidental' meetings or talk of their deeds or beauty. Others tried to hide what they wanted, only a casual mention of their name or an invitation to a future event.

Ma had been very busy since his stewardship began. Horribly so.

She thought seventeen was too old to not already be betrothed. Her life had been in Wylow, the nearest town, before moving here with his father, they had married young and adored the life they chose. The notion of any other path simply couldn't be contemplated. He was quite certain she had already picked out names for the children she hoped he would produce.

He didn't blame her and knew from talk with Kreg or Lusha that other parents were the same, but it still stung. He wasn't sure if Rightwy would be where he wanted to stay forever; the whole of Brodanna was beyond its little walls. So many things to discover...

He hadn't noticed the little wooden structures of the village pass him by, even the usual aroma of the small market failed to attract his attention. His eyes were too busy glancing towards the iron gates that marked the entrance and exit to Rightwy.

The surrounding wall blocked what was beyond. How many times had he been through those gates? How many times had he even ventured into Wylow?

Far from enough.

It would be worth it. The staying. For Ma, and for Herman's training. Others would have come from the Black Lands or as far as the Squi Mountains for such a chance.

The world would be waiting afterwards, and he needed to remember that.

A drink would do him some good. He could ignore the chants or suggestions of courtship. Kreg would be full of stories about his day and Len's ferocious temper. He would want to know about Ivloch's 'patient' wait for Reeves' decision. He had asked every moon if Herman had accepted him yet, refusing to believe, even for a moment, that he would not be successful.

No doubt he would find it an excellent excuse for several drinks and telling anyone who dared to bother them to go the hell away.

For such a small man, he had an incredibly big mouth, and an even sharper tongue.

The Seven Whiskers was a sorry looking place. Paint had come off its sign, so it only read 'H S Whisk". Boards were over the windows and a smashed bench provided the only outside seating, unless you were willing to sit on the grass. Today was not a good day for sitting on the ground. Later in summer and the awakening maybe, but winter had refused to release its clutches, and it would be too cold, even for a man of Ivloch's size.

One of the locals, without a daughter thankfully, stepped outside for a smoke as he went through the wooden door. Ivloch greeted him warmly but didn't share his news. Telling anyone before Kreg would be quite the insult and he wouldn't hear the end of it for moon turns. If ever.

Inside was as forlorn as the outside. Candles hung low from the ceiling, providing the only light over twelve dirty and dishevelled tables. Not enough stools were scattered around them, they were only occasionally used by patrons, so never replaced. Ivloch had seen five meet their end in a mighty brawl on his last visit.

The bar was on the furthest side from the door, higher wooden seats along its edge. Crazy Shaun was sat at one talking to himself, or the voices he claimed to hear. Some thought he was a lunatic, others whispered he could talk to The Unforgiven. The truth was he drank to wipe away the moons since his daughter had gone missing three summers ago. Ivloch had been good friends with Una when they were children.

He walked over to Shaun and patted him on the back before asking about his day. Shaun never gave much of an answer but there always seemed to be a light in his eyes, as if he appreciated Ivloch's efforts.

Shaun shuffled off towards the dirt covered bathroom and Ivloch took a seat at the other end of the bar. The landlord Eris was talking to a man in a giant straw hat at one of the tables, but Ivloch was happy to wait. Kreg would still be some time.

Eris waved to him as he watched and motioned drinking from a tankard. Ivloch wasn't quite sure what he meant until he looked around.

She was beautiful. Nothing like any of the women he had dreamed of.

Her hair reached past her shoulders, its vibrant blonde the colour of summer's golden glow. Her gown hung off her delicate shoulders but covered her arms in their entirety.

She stared at him with arresting emerald green eyes. He wondered why and smoothed out the creases in his white tunic. Her pale fingers began to tap on the bar in impatience. It took him longer than it should to realise she was waiting for him to order a drink.

Eris' motion. *Oh, to The Transmitter.*

"Are you going to order something, or would you rather die of thirst? It's my first day and I'm not sure I'm prepared for that much of a clean-up job." Her voice was unfamiliar; he knew she wasn't from Rightwy. He would have remembered such a woman and the hint of an accent suggested she hadn't come from the nearby Wylow either.

"Err…ale. I drink ale."

She rolled her eyes and moved to pour the drink. Her long skirt following in her wake. Ivloch cursed himself for such a ludicrous response. She plonked a tankard before him, dark liquid sploshing over the sides.

"Thank you." He found coins in his pockets and passed them over.

"I'm glad you finally noticed I'm here."

"It's been a long day. I'm sorry. My name is Ivloch."

"That's nice Ivloch."

She said nothing else as she danced away to serve Shaun, but Ivloch remained thinking about her as he sipped the ale. It tasted a little sweeter than usual.

***

It was only Kreg's arrival that provided her name.

He bristled in, the door banging behind him. His muddy brown hair looked greasy but he wore a smile on his dirt smeared face. The slight limp he had developed the previous awakening slowed him as he made his way to the stool.

The limp's origin had been a course for great gossip across Rightwy. Kreg adamantly refused to confirm or deny any theory.

"Ruddy day, man, I tell you. Len's a madman." He wriggled as he sat, determined to be as comfortable as possible. "This ruddy cold, it makes my leg ache like nothing else. I need a massage and a hot spring."

The woman was there, a glass of wine being passed in Kreg's direction.

"Oh Becca, you beautiful darling. I knew I was right to tell Eris to hire you." He grinned and sipped. "Ivloch, have you met her? Isn't she wonderful? We played cards when she came in and she thrashed me! Me! Can you imagine?"

He couldn't. Kreg's winning exploits at cards were renowned throughout the village, to the point that most refused to play with him and lose their coin.

Kreg kept talking but Ivloch could barely focus, the name Becca was springing through his mind.

It seemed to suit her.

He listened sporadically as Kreg described how delighted he was to have been here and met her first, that Eris had obviously only given her work because he suggested it. He was very keen to mention how Ivloch missed all the good things looking after that Ma of his.

Usually he would disagree, but Becca made him believe Kreg had a point. There really was a first time for everything.

Becca moved away again after laughing far too much at Kreg's jokes. Ivloch tried not to be annoyed at him. Kreg might like this woman but he would have no romantic interest in her. Only Esmerelda had Kreg's heart.

He finally calmed down enough to tell his friend about the apprenticeship. Kreg seemed to forget all about the pain in his leg as he jumped off the stall and proceeded to whoop with happiness. Even whilst standing, he only reached a seated Ivloch's shoulder.

The sheer excitement radiating from him whipped the whole tavern into a frenzy. Kreg took it upon himself to tell all twelve inhabitants exactly how wonderful Ivloch was and what a coveted thing he had managed.

Becca sidled up to him and passed him a shot of Black Lands Yula. The sheer iridescent liquid glinted up at him. One drink of it cost more than he earnt in a quarter moon turn.

"From the boss, big man. Guess you're not as incompetent as I feared."

That was the compliment he took home with him, as he stumbled most of the way. Yula was guaranteed to get any man drunk.

He clung to the words as Ma raged against Herman's teachings and screeched about him wasting time with 'that no good Kreg'.

"Just settle down, son. Become a craftsman and maybe marry Livia or Teninya. It'll be much better."

The alcohol and his good mood helped make ignoring her even easier than usual.

Three

Herman was not a kind teacher.

He worked him from dawn to dusk, even when Master Reeves came to watch and barked loudly about needing his laundry folded and a distinct lack of crabble leaf tea.

Three moon turns had passed since the training began, summer grew riper with each passing second, winter an old memory. Every single moon he had come to Master Reeves' house, helped him run errands and then found Herman. Bruises coated his long legs, half of his chest was black and Kreg had found the cut across his temple hilarious.

He was loving every second of it.

The large body The Transmitter had gifted him with had always been gangly until now. Muscles had started to develop in places he hadn't known they could. Every morning he woke a little brighter, his body slowly aching less and less. Even Master Reeves had commented on his physique changing. "Hmm, carry on like this and I'll have to stop calling you boy." His life had changed, but he was much the happier for it.

Visiting Kreg as soon as he finished had become a tradition. The Seven Whiskers took most of his pitiful pay, but he didn't think he would have it any other way.

As he cleaned the sword Herman had best him with only moments before, he was particularly excited to get there this moon. Lusha was visiting again. His last planned one had only been for a few hours, barely enough time to have more than one drink.

Becca hadn't even been working. He was very keen to find out his cousin's opinion of her.

He had amassed a significant ledger on Becca Jenns.

Becca was a year older than him, born in the awakening, just as he had been. She had a sister and a brother, which she seemed reluctant to discuss, but always glowed with pride when she did. He was convinced she lived outside Rightwy and found that fascinating. Her hair was always worn down and she always appeared to wear a form of green in her outfits.

Esmerelda loved her. Kreg's wife took to her instantly and the two became fast friends. As a great respecter of 'Relda, Ivloch was entirely convinced this was a good thing.

Daydreams about double dates and visiting one another in later life, with hordes of children at their feet had occurred on three occasions, but he tried to keep them to a minimum. So far, he had not shared any of these wishes with Kreg who would have bellowed in laughter and demanded he actually speak to Becca before he got carried away.

Talking to her was the problem.

She spoke freely to Kreg, Shaun, Eris or any other patron. Just not him. He didn't know if he had greatly offended her or she simply didn't like him. He asked once, but she just shook her head and found something else to do across the bar. There had to be a reason she avoided him, and he was determined to find it.

Lusha was a favourite in the village. A hero willing to fight for the handsome and wonderful King. He was defending the Queen's new baby, didn't you know? Lusha would help. He would charm her and then even after he disappeared off in that black and red uniform, Becca would have warmed to him.

They would be friends.

He wasn't sure he wanted anything more, as doting as he knew he had become. The idea had started to scare him, not just with Becca, although, he only had eyes for her, but with anyone.

The stronger the training with Herman had made him, the more men suddenly had daughters. The accidental meetings or girls wanting to follow him and talk about their cooking skills had tripled. Kreg found it hilarious.

"They're all ruddy over you! It's like they've never seen a man before. Ruddy heck, if they only knew what a fool you were 'ey?"

Becca had laughed when Kreg said it. She didn't seem impressed with the women suddenly sat at the bar fluttering their eyelashes either. The memory confused him.

He had let his thoughts wander as he worked and it was late by the time Master Reeves finally said he could leave.

"That's enough now boy. You have your first and only rest moon tomorrow. Don't waste it on any nonsense and don't come back to me tired. You work, boy. There will be much tidying to be done. I'll make a mess for you to clean before Herman has at you. You wait, boy."

Ivloch was sceptical. Reeves, despite his age, eye-sight and lack of agility, happened to be one of the cleanest people he had ever met. He thought he would probably have a fit if he walked into the Seven Whiskers. Even with Becca's attempts to clean, it still resembled a sour smelling hovel.

Kreg was laughing at a table with Lusha, 'Relda and Becca when he arrived. Lusha jumped up to embrace him and Becca's eyes shifted with suspicion. He sat with them and 'Relda pushed a cup of wine towards him.

"I can't believe how strong you look cousin! You'll be nearly as much of a man as me soon." Lusha didn't mince his words. "We've been up in the Spykelands this summer, Jefferson says there are Wielders causing havoc all over the place. Bloody nuisance really. Best thing he has done, starting to hunt them."

He hated the way Lusha spoke as if the King was his friend when Ivloch doubted he had even met the man. He also didn't agree with his constantly stated prejudice against the Powered, but that wouldn't stop him. It never did.

"Must we start with all the Wielder this, wonderful King crap that, already?" Esmerelda was a User. Ivloch had known since Kreg met her, but otherwise the secret was hers. Her power only ever used in front of people she truly trusted. Her mother had warned her dangerous times were coming and it was something she refused to let herself forget.

"Oh Esme'…" Lusha sighed.

She hated being called Esme and pursed her lips accordingly.

"Are you really going to remain so on the fence? It's the ruddy Wielders that got us stuck here. Wielders that destroyed the Seven Worlds. The Unforgiven caused a war, destroyed our greatest Queen. I thought women's issues are, you know, your thing."

Ivloch winced as Lusha stopped speaking and drained his cup. This wasn't quite going to be the evening he had hoped for. Lusha could be wonderful but he needed to learn his audience. Esmerelda had turned red in the face, anger written across every feature.

"How wonderful it must be to believe your opinion is so much more valid than everyone else's. Did your wonderful King tell you what he does to those Users he captures? Or how he has never publicly condemned The Unforgiven?" Becca spoke with such passion that Ivloch moved back in his chair and let out a long breath. Esmerelda clapped, but Becca paid no attention as she left the table and returned to the bar.

Lusha dropped the subject after her departure but Ivloch couldn't force himself to relax. Questions came about the work with Herman and he answered, but the words fell flat.

Kreg drank and joked enough for the both of them. Esmerelda seemed as tense as he was and kept disappearing to talk with Becca.

He couldn't tell if they were upset or just riled, but the looks sent in his direction were far from pleasant.

He went to the bar with trepidation in every step.

"What do you want? Ale? Wine? Do you drink anything else?"

"Well…sometimes. I've never ordered anything else here though, I suppose."

"You're fussy. I've noticed. Shame the same can't be said about your choice of friends."

"Becca…"

"Don't Becca me. We are not even friends, Ivloch Youchnore."

She slammed a tankard before him and dismissed herself, Esmerelda looked on nervously and shrugged.

It was only as he sat back down that he noticed he had never told her his surname. Clearly someone had, or perhaps she had asked.

Becca left before Eris wanted to close up and didn't say goodbye to even 'Relda, who watched her walk away in dismay.

Kreg and Lusha were off ordering drinks and singing. Even Ivloch was starting to feel rather merry.

"I worry about Becca," 'Relda declared, staring intently at him.

"I don't think she likes me much."

Esmerelda laughed. "It never fails to amaze me how little men know about women sometimes."

***

The next morning, he took Ma to the market.

She seemed delighted with the outing, even more so when everyone stopped them to chat. It was quite astounding how many young women she wanted to introduce him to. Ivloch made sure to smile and nod when it was deemed appropriate but gave her little other hope.

"Do you not like women, Ivloch? You must tell me!" She seemed very impatient as he walked her home.

"I do Ma, but that's not the point, is it?"

"I only worry about you. When I've gone chasing after your father in the next life, won't you be so lonely?"

Talk of his father always reached the more tender places in his heart and he was certain she knew it. Still, it worked, and he promised her he would consider the idea when the training with Herman was over.

"Oh Ivloch, you mean it?" He said he did. He didn't know if he'd told the truth, but the words sent her happily in to her afternoon slumber.

As she slept, he dashed for the door. He took special effort to change in to his favourite tunic and the brown cape Lusha had brought him back from Tonkara. His shoulder length blond hair was tied at the top of his head and he was sure he looked much better than he did after a moons work.

Not that it would matter. She wouldn't care how he looked, she probably never did. He just hoped it would make him feel slightly better about the whole situation.

If he hurried, he would have longer to apologise to her before he had to go and meet Kreg and Lusha for their hunting party. He hated such a thing, one of the few skills he had never mastered, but neither man would want to cancel the trip.

Becca was behind the bar, in a blue tunic this time. The usual cosmetics on her cheeks were missing and her golden locks looked slightly dishevelled.

She seemed to noticeably groan as she saw him.

"What now? If your friend's missing, then I'm not the killer. I wouldn't want to get my hands dirty."

"Cousin actually."

She handed him a tankard he hadn't asked for, but he accepted it without complaint. "Even worse if you're related."

"Is it? You can't choose your family, only your friends. I came to apologise for him. He has his own…way of looking at the world, but I don't agree with him and I want you to know that."

She stopped her frantic cleaning of the bar and considered him, her head tilting slightly to the side. The tunic covered her arms again, he wondered if there was a reason they were always under wraps.

"Why do you care what I think, Ivloch Youchnore?"

A million answers came to him, all too revealing or with not enough weight.

"You're different to the people I've met before and I respect you. This isn't about you though. I wouldn't want anyone to believe I thought like that."

"Esmerelda." Her answer shocked him. Had 'Relda told her? He knew they were friends but to trust her with that secret after how paranoid she was… "I guessed. She confirmed. I'm glad you care about your friends, Ivloch. It's a pretty underrated pastime."

"I'd like us to be friends, Becca." He meant it. Even if he ignored the way a room always seemed brighter with her in it.

"Careful what you wish for, Youchnore."

The ale he had just brought to his mouth missed and fell down his shirt. Becca leaned over and wiped the splash which had landed on his cheek and he tried not to blush.

"You should think about a beard. It would suit the whole warrior thing you're growing in to."

She walked away humming, but he smiled.

The afternoon with Kreg and Lusha didn't seem so bad after all.

Four

He scratched the hair on his chin as Herman looked up at him.

"I am impressed. We are done for today. You should celebrate." The tall bald man uttered little else as he got up from the sandy floor and dusted himself off. Ivloch knew not to say thank you, Herman was not keen on such niceties and simply tilted his head before walking away.

Four further moon turns it had taken; but he had succeeded. He had knocked Herman to the floor with his blade. The blade, Inferno's Kiss, was gifted to him by Master Reeves on his birth moon; it was his new, most treasured possession. It was a beautiful weapon, made of steel from The Black Lands, and suited his size perfectly.

"If you're going to learn to fight, then you ought to have a weapon, boy, hadn't you? Here, take it. I can't lift the thing anymore and all it does is collect dust and make a mess, saves you cleaning, boy."

He had hugged the old man, much to his dismay. "Oh boy, what are you doing? I've given you a sword, not a Darkstar! Off with you!" Reeves insisted he leave training early that day, so he doubted he was as insulted as he had pretended.

He was very glad he was also leaving early this moon, The Seven Whiskers was having a party for the Prince's first year. He couldn't say he much cared about the child, but the celebration meant everyone would be in rather high spirits and that was always welcome.

Lusha hadn't returned since the last visit, and for that, he was grateful.

It had allowed him to strengthen his friendship with Becca.

She had visited the market with him and watched one of his training sessions. Spending more time with her, even celebrating their birth in a joint gathering, had left him incredibly happy.

"I'm glad I gave you a chance Youchnore," she had declared, making him beam.

He even thought he had caught her looking at his beard. He woke each morning hoping it had grown, dismayed that it took so long. Ma hated it and raged each evening that he should remove it, or risk spending his life alone and loveless.

"You look like a beggar from the Spykelands! Cut your hair, get rid of the face fluff and you'll find a pretty girl to settle down with."

His blonde hair had grown out down his back. He wore it in a tight bun for training and let it loose for the evenings. Becca and Esmerelda had even decided to braid it one summer night when they drank Cactle Juice on the grass. He hated the drink but was determined to broaden his horizons and try every odd concoction Becca made him.

"How will you ever know what you like if you don't give things a go? You can't be so stubborn!"

He was trying not to be and if nothing else, it seemed to make her smile.

Ivloch could only hope she would be at the party.

He waved goodbye to Master Reeves and headed in the direction of the tavern, trying not to let his thoughts run away from him, but failing.

There had been days recently where she disappeared without warning. Two or three shifts just missed. She would come back looking grim and tired; refusing to ever tell him or Kreg where she had been.

"We all have secrets Ivloch, let me keep mine. Please."

He did, but he worried for her. There had been a bruise on her neck once. One she promised no lover had made. If she had a partner, that was fine, he could have accepted the news, but not one that would hurt her.

Another return had left her looking pale and sickly; she even became dizzy during her shift.

She was a mystery that he never stopped wanting to investigate.

He was acutely aware that at some point he had fallen hopelessly in love with her. Even Kreg had noticed. He also knew himself well enough to understand that if nothing happened between them, he could cope. He would rather live as her friend, than nothing at all. Some people just made life better by be being in it.

***

Esmerelda was storming away as he reached the Whiskers. The awakening heat, the last of summer, had already made him break out in a sweat and the usual muddy path had turned to fine dust. Her curly red hair was glowing in the sunlight and her face held an expression that sent a wave of fear through him.

'Relda, are you alright?" She paced up and down before him, her right hand stroking the hem of her thin cotton black robe.

"I hate him, Ivloch. He's too ruddy scared to live our lives, but won't do anything to stand up to the threat either!" A wail of frustration erupted from her lips. "How do you all do it? Pretend our world isn't falling apart? How do you sleep at night? He won't try! He won't even let me be happy with the mess we have."

Ivloch wasn't completely sure what she meant but he could take a good guess; it was an old argument he had witnessed between 'Relda and Kreg on many an occasion. "You know it's not that simple 'Relda. You know he's scared of both options; he just needs some time to work out which one he can face."

"Why one? Why does there have to be a choice to what I want? Why should he need time whilst I'm just left waiting, fearing for a life I'm unable to live!" Her hands moved with her words and she huffed in his direction. "You know…don't bother. You'll just be like him and you won't ruddy understand. Just go, get drunk and live on your daydreams," Esmerelda raged. "Becca's not there, just so you know."

She flounced away. Not in the direction of the house she shared with Little Kreg, but towards the village gate. He knew she was prone to long solo walks to nurse her power and calm herself.

He took a deep breath and carried on towards the tavern.

If 'Relda had been in that kind of mood, he doubted Kreg would be in a better one.

Kreg was already incredibly inebriated. Eris moved a line of shot cups away from the small man as Ivloch found him, sat alone at one of the messy tables. He was running a hand through his already greying dark hair and ushering a newly refilled glass of wine towards his mouth.

"What happened? I saw 'Relda." He sat down after asking Eris, as he usually did, to put his weapon behind the bar. The innkeeper never allowed weapons of any kind on his patrons, something Ivloch considered wise.

"She's gone mad." Kreg sobbed and refused to lift his attention from the wine.

Ivloch thought as passionate as Esmerelda could be sometimes, she was certainly not mad. He cleared his throat and prompted Kreg to continue. He shakily looked around the tavern to make sure nobody could overhear them. In this state Kreg would not be adept at keeping her secret.

"She's ruddy well decided she either wants a baby or to go hunt down Kara's ruddy Guild. Can you imagine? Us as resistance fighters? Thinks we should stop ignoring all the bad things brewing and either settle down or go get ourselves ruddy hunted." Kreg downed the wine and winced at the taste. "I mean, what's a man to do Ivloch? I ruddy love her, I do. She's everything I ever wanted and more, but that's not a choice!"

Ivloch tried to bite his tongue and allow his drunk friend to finish.

"I like it here, with you and even ruddy Len. We get by. We do our thing. Someone's just put lofty ideas in her head and taken advantage of how paranoid her Mama was. This King might be a bugger and the wind might be blowing against Users, but it won't come to anything. Never ruddy does, does it?" The big maple eyes which dominated Kreg's narrow face looked at him with hope.

Ivloch wasn't sure if Kreg wanted him to answer honestly, or if he just sought reassurance. He opted for picking up the wine glass and meandering towards Eris at the bar. Some time to think of an answer would be best, to mull over Kreg's rant.

The wine went down well as he returned. Kreg shuffled uncomfortably on his stool. He would know him well enough to know he had needed a chance to appropriate the correct response; one that would be fair to both Kreg and 'Relda.

"You love her because of who she is, and she's always been one of extremes. You can't fault her for caring now. Why not have a baby? Why not join The Guild? You say nothing ever comes of it, but they've started hunting Users, Kreg. Lusha says so. The King is causing hatred and fear and it's spreading quicker than rumours in Rightwy!" Kreg tried to pout but ended up laughing, as Ivloch had hoped. "'Relda is wonderful, don't let you being scared, or worried, or nervous, ruin that, because I will have no sympathy for you, let me tell you!"

It was true. The people had spent so long being angry about not inheriting the powers they believed should have been their own by birth right, that they were more than happy to blame those who did have such a gift. Even men like Lusha, who weren't bad and hadn't believed such nonsense, had started to align with the King's thinking.

Lusha had dreamed of one day discovering he was a User. Ivloch could remember the two of them running across the market as children, Lusha raising his arms and screaming that he was casting an incantation on Ivloch. He had believed that's how it worked back then. Only Esmerelda had been able to show him how Wielding truly worked.

Kreg drank the wine and stomped his feet on the stone floor.

"Can you imagine me with a baby? Or smithing for The Guild? Maybe I should talk to her. I have to work with Len until I'm trained but maybe…maybe we could ruddy see if it means that much!" He hooted and patted Ivloch's back. Kreg had always responded well to Ivloch's advice, he just hoped this time, it wasn't the alcohol talking.

Their conversation ended at the right time as the door opened and revellers from the earlier Prince's parade burst through. The tavern was suddenly filled to the brim and Eris was haphazardly handing out drinks to everyone from the other side of the bar. It was quite impressive how many people wanted to celebrate the birthday of Hamill Landress, the royal baby that no person from Rightwy had ever seen. Any excuse for a party...

"Oh laddie, we're in for a night!" The little man pounded his fists on the table and screeched before jumping up to greet Livia Llanos. Ivloch was entirely impressed he didn't topple on to the floor considering how intoxicated he was.

Livia also worked for Len and had become Kreg's only workplace ally against the older man's temper. She was tall, much taller than Kreg, with a mass of brown curls, a tiny nose and russet skin. Her inappropriate jokes were discussed as much as her thick curves, by anyone who met her. It was only the men she caught talking of the latter that she challenged to a fight. One she always seemed to win. It was said her nose bent to the right due to one such brawl; Ivloch was glad he had never seen the other party.

He thought Becca would approve of Livia; another wish that she was present.

She would have known how to handle Kreg immediately and probably calmed 'Relda down.

But Becca Jenns wasn't here. She was off with her secrets and The Seven Whiskers would be far from her mind. Just like he was.

Ivloch couldn't help but notice Livia's lilac summer gown or the way she smiled at him.

Livia had been the only girl he had ever kissed.

She made no secret of her desire for him and whilst he had been terrified, her quick-witted conversation and general ease had relaxed him enough to reciprocate on that occasion. Livia was lovely, a friend even, but he had told her he wasn't ready for anything more. She had understood and told him to focus on what he did want; the stewardship with Reeves. She had walked him to Reeves' house that first day, when he had been filled with nerves about working for such a man, a time before training with Herman had even been a possibility.

"I like the beard and I need to see this sword Kreg has whittled on about for so long," Livia proclaimed, sliding into the seat beside him.

Kreg blushed and rushed off to fetch more drinks. It was rather nice to know his friend was proud of him. The thought made him smile as he eased into conversation with Livia. Perhaps the evening could be salvaged after all...

Five

Livia lay in bed next to him and he didn't recognise the tiny orange - walled room.

It took moments before he recalled the night before…

The dancing. The constant drinks. Sitting on the grass with Liv and telling her about training...

Oh, to the Transmitter…he had spoken about his feelings for Becca.

"I love her, but she wants to be friends and I'm alright with that, but I don't know, does it stop me from seeing anyone else? It shouldn't, but I'm unsure, maybe there's something wrong with me," he had slurred, and Livia had been there. All kisses and tongues and wetness.

He had gone back with her, to the little hut she shared with another work friend. Fear had gripped him as she pulled off his tunic and ran her cold hands through his golden hair.

"Just breathe. It's better if you relax and if you try it with a friend." Soft kisses had run down his neck, dark hands visited places nowhere but his own had ever been. "It doesn't have to mean anything more than what it is, Ivloch. If you want to, we can?"

He had wanted to, and they had.

It had been different to what he expected. Nicer. Noisier.

Livia rolled over, the fur covering pulled to her neck. He was rather glad they also covered his modesty. He had been braver with the drink, but he would turn scarlet if she witnessed him uncovered in the light of day.

"Are you alright? You don't regret it?" She spoke softly as she stretched her shapely legs out.

"I don't. It was… brilliant. Thank you, Liv. Is that the right thing to say? I don't really know." He took in a breath and allowed himself to meet her eyes. "Don't hate me."

A cackle came from her throat as she removed herself from the covers and the mess of the bed. She searched for her discarded clothes which had been unceremoniously tossed across the floor.

"That's a fine thing to say, Ivloch. It's all alright and there's no hate. I had a good evening, and we're still friends? Aren't we?"

He nodded, worry and confusion mixing with a hesitant wish from his body to experience more of what it had the previous night.

Another memory came, from before the kiss. Him wailing about Becca and Livia talking about how her heart had somehow started to want Len and she couldn't stop it. Len was adamant she was too young and far too foolish to get involved with him.

"You love Len." He whispered the fact more to himself, but Livia heard and threw yesterday's dress at his head.

"Let's not repeat that little nugget, and I won't remind you of your Becca! Seem like a deal?" She dressed. New garments produced from the small wooden unit that took up the rest of the room, and sat back down on the bed. She grinned again as she reached for his hand. "We're friends and we were both sad and a little lonely. If we can make each other feel a little better in this messed up world with no damage, then isn't that a good thing?"

He supposed it was, but sheepishly inquired whether she took a birth elixir. A chortle this time. "I'm a big lady, Ivloch. I can handle that stuff, don't you worry. You should probably get dressed and go and retrieve your sword though."

He had left the blade with Eris. What a drunken fool he was.

He hopped out of Liv's bed; all embarrassment forgotten. She giggled and chucked his clothes towards him.

Master Reeves had given him that weapon. The look of disapproval on the old man's face if he ever heard what had happened... Herman's rage. Ivloch wasn't sure if he would be able to live with letting them both down.

The goodbye felt awkward, but he didn't let himself overthink as he sprinted towards the Whiskers.

He had to retrieve Inferno's Kiss...

He was terribly out of breath by the time he approached the closed inn. Becca was outside, wearing the same outfit she had worn the day he met her. He waved but she didn't wave back, her face remained sombre, harder than usual, with a twinge of pity in her iridescent eyes.

"Ivloch, where the ruddy hell have you been?" She looked him up and down. At the tunic not quite done up correctly, at the hair which hadn't seen a brush and the straggly beard which puffed out from his big cheeks.

A crimson streak seemed to flash across her face but mellowed quickly, as she stepped towards him.

"I'm so sorry. They've been looking for you. Something's happened…"
She told him and held him tight as he sobbed on to her shoulder.

He later thought the scene must have looked ridiculous. He was three times her size and weeping, yet she was the only thing keeping him upright.

That moon, he didn't care. There was very little that mattered at all.

Six

Kreg and Esmerelda had found her at first light when they sought Ivloch to tell him their good news. Ma had died on her chaise, her favourite parchment book in hand.

The town Healer said it would have been quick and as peaceful as these things ever were. None of that made it any better.

Ivloch let Becca come with him to see her body and do what must be done. She held his hand tightly and let him release all the sorrow inside. The guilt remained.

Ma looked so tiny laid out on the wooden slab, all ready for burial next to The Transmitter's temple.

"It's not your fault, Ivloch. They said you couldn't have done anything if you were there." Becca stroked his hair as she spoke.

"I could have said goodbye. She should never have been alone." She put her arms around him, and he leant into the warmth.

Becca came back to the little house that now belonged to him, and they picked out Ma's best dress for her to wear. As Becca folded it up, ready to leave, he realised he had never told Ma that she existed. She may just be his friend, but he thought the two would have got on. Becca would have laughed and been able to respond to Ma's taunts with her own. He cried again.

The small service happened in the afternoon. Kreg and Esmerelda loyally on his left. Becca to his right, only stepping away when Livia came to hug him. Somehow, Becca knew who he had been with the night before.

Herman came, an odd sight not in his armour, Master Reeves limping at his side. They hadn't known Ma but Ivloch was touched they made the trip.

"You rest, boy. Take a few moons. Cuddle your lady. I'll make Herman stay and teach you, boy, for longer if you need it." Becca had turned scarlet at Reeve's suggestion, but Ivloch had just hugged him. Reeves didn't object this time.

Other villagers paid their respects. A line of well-wishers and condolences until his hand felt dry and awkward from shaking so many others. Most prayers were uttered to the Transmitter but Ivloch heard Esmerelda, Becca and a select few whisper their words to Kara.

He didn't ask anyone to take care of Ma's soul; she would already been dominating the next life.

Eris finally stepped in and announced they would all have a drink at The Whiskers in Ma's honour. An overwhelming gratitude to the tavern owner coursed through him. The chance of a few moments away from strangers' glares was the biggest blessing he could have been given.

Becca didn't work but stayed by his side. 'Relda and Kreg did the same and they all found a spot on the grass, away from the pressure of inside.

Livia kept her distance. He saw her only once glance at Becca holding his hand and smile. He thought she saw more to the gesture than there was, but he was grateful for her understanding.

They stayed until Eris wanted to close.

"We should head off now," Esmerelda sighed and inched closer to ruffle his mane of hair. "You come by tomorrow for breakfast and take care of yourself, big man. We love you and we're here."

Kreg repeated the sentiment, a little nervously but with just as much heart. Ivloch didn't remember they had news to give him until after they had walked away.

Then it was only her left.

He looked towards the direction of home and not Becca. He didn't want to see the pity on her face or have her ask about Ma. He missed her already, an ache that wasn't going away and there had been so many tears. So many 'what-if's' despite the Healer's words. They had been wrong before.

Home would be lonely without her. Even the nagging. He never thought he would miss the nagging. Had she thought of him before it happened? If there had been time?

Her words that day in the market came to him… 'Without me, won't you be lonely?' He would. Horribly so.

"Eris is lending me a room in the tavern tonight so I'm going to walk you home." Becca took his arm and yanked him forward.

"Aren't men meant to walk women home?" He asked, as he matched her pace.

"So some say. They also claim women are weak creatures, men can be evil, and nobody can take care of themselves or deal with their actions. You've had a bad day and there are much worse things in the world than in Rightwy. I'm walking you home, Ivloch."

"Women aren't weak, some men can be horrid, and everyone struggles to deal with their choices sometimes. Don't you?"

The moon glinted in her eyes as she stared up towards it. "I used to, but then I decided to do some things that were right, things I could be proud of, even if I am foolish." She tucked her hair behind her ears with her free hand. "Did you enjoy last night? I hope I wasn't in Livia's way today."

Ivloch paused on the cobblestones. If he carried on, they would reach his house soon and he wasn't ready. He spied the small wooden bench, which sat by Rightwy's only pond and paced towards it, hoping Becca would follow. She groaned but did as he hoped. They sat in silence, admiring the moonlight glinting off the black water.

He needed to talk; even if it wasn't wise. It had been an emotional moon; one of change and loss and it made him reckless.

Time was limited and often so cruel.

He wanted to answer her question about Livia. "I had a nice evening, but I won't be doing it again."

"Sex? I guess that's fine. Some people don't enjoy it. You have to do whatever makes you happy."

"That's…that isn't what I meant. Sex is nice. I like it. Do you not? There is nothing wrong with not liking it, but I think I do. I meant…" He hated his rambling but couldn't stop himself. "I meant with Livia. We're friends and going to stay that way."

Becca clasped her hands in her lap. Her eyes were intent on the water. "Does she know? I thought maybe…"

"She knows. I think…" He gulped. What he was about to say could ruin their friendship. It could make him go home and feel lonelier than he already would without Ma. "I think that Livia's heart belongs to someone else too."

Becca tore her scrutiny from the pond and turned it squarely on him. "Ivloch, are you trying to tell me that you had sex with a woman, but you love me? Because that is the most messed up thing I've ever heard, and you have no idea how many ridiculous things I get told." She stood up, paced, anger radiating from her small frame. "That is not romantic. It is not loving. It's crap and it's stupid and it won't get you anywhere with me or any other woman in Brodanna or the ruddy Seven Worlds."

"No. I didn't mean that. I did have sex with her, and I am in love with you but… I wasn't thinking of you. It was what both me and Livia needed at the time and you've made it clear you want to be nothing more than friends and that's fine…" She looked unsure but had stopped walking. "It is, it never used to be, but it is. I think you're wonderful though, Becca, and until I stop that, I'm not going to fall for Livia or anyone else. That's my issue and not yours. I know that. I'm not a monster and I care for Liv but we both understood the situation."

Her legs carried her back to the bench, her shoulders hunched.

He felt like a fool and he knew everything had come out wrong, but couldn't regret it. It might have been the wine or the grief, but the air had needed to clear if they were ever to be the true friends Becca wanted them to be.

"I care about you, Ivloch. This was meant to be a job, some extra money and a viable cover. You and 'Relda and Kreg. I never expected this and it's a complication." She tried to take his hand again, but he pulled it back.

"A cover?"

"I can't tell you, so don't ask. It's bigger than me or you. Even Rightwy." Her fingers brushed his leg. "I have to go away again tomorrow for a while. There isn't any way I can change it, but I'm glad I could be here for you this moon. It meant a lot to me, Ivloch Youchnore."

"Where do you go, Becca?"

"I would tell you if I could."

She leant over and kissed him. It wasn't the sloppy thing him and Livia had been. There was no drunken urgency or haunted horror behind the deed. It was soft and slow and she reached for his face, her hand gliding down his cheek.

"We have to be friends, Ivloch, but you have a place in my heart, even if you aren't meant to."

He didn't move as she pulled away.

She was going to leave, and he knew it. There was no way he could stop her and if he tried, she would hate him. Resentment was a hard thing to lose.

He wanted to know her secrets, nearly as much as he wanted to see Ma again, but he didn't *need* to know them.

If he cared for her then he could respect her wishes, even if it would leave him wondering. Watching the door of The Whiskers and hoping a petite blonde, with such wonderful eyes, would walk through the door…

"Do you like the beard? You never told me."

She was about to walk away, but she turned back. Her hand returned to his face, mingling with the thick white hairs he had grown at her suggestion.

"I love it, Ivloch Youchnore. You take care of yourself and I'll see you soon."

"Promise?"

"I never make promises, it's not fair on the people they can't be kept for, but I vow to do my best."

He watched her go all the way back to the tavern before he decided to finish his journey, to an all too empty home.

Seven

Becca didn't return in the two moon-turns it took to finish his apprenticeship.

"Herman says you are good fighter now, boy, better than him maybe, one day. Maybe I call you man now," Reeves stammered, reaching up to pat his big shoulders.

Ivloch had beamed with pride, despite the bittersweet knowledge he had succeeded without Ma. She would have been proud; in between the nagging. He made sure to visit her small grave and tell her Reeves' words, with Esmerelda at his side.

Kreg, Relda, Eris and Livia threw him a congratulations party in the Whiskers which all the villagers attended. Liv had been a good friend to him.

'Relda had eventually told him the news she and Kreg had planned to, the morning of Ma's passing. His old friend had finally consented to have a family with her. So much so, that now, Kreg wouldn't stop talking about wanting a baby, despite 'Relda insisting he keep his mouth shut until they conceived. It made his heart warm, even on the darker days.

Talk of The Guild still crossed Relda's lips. Kreg thought the child would mean an end to it, but Ivloch firmly believed she would get what she wanted; even with an infant at their side.

He had taken on a few bounty contracts over in Wylow since Herman left. Small things, thief catching mostly, but the work kept him almost content. It paid well, more coin than he had seen. Eris told him to go to one of the cities, even the Spykelands, to earn more and see the world, but he hadn't made the leap yet.

He wanted to say it was for his friends. To know if Little Kreg and Relda would have a red-haired baby as dauntless as its mother, or if Livia would ever win Len round to her way of thinking but…that was only part of it.

She had not promised to return, but he hoped.

He had never known Becca to try her best and not succeed. Still, her absence made each passing week a little harder for him.

***

He was at the market with Livia when Relda found him.

Winter's oncoming chill forced them both to wrap up warmly in several thick layers; but he didn't mind. The past moon turn had meant he spent quite a lot of time in Wylow and some friendly company was exactly what he needed. Life outside Rightwy's walls was everything he had wanted; but far lonelier than he had ever anticipated.

"Ivloch! Liv! You have to come to The Whiskers! Me and Kreg have something to tell you!"

He paid for the breeches he had been eyeing before they made their way to the tavern. Relda had already disappeared off, to find Kreg, or race to the pub, he was quite unsure.

"What do you think it is?" Livia pouted. Len had told her to move on. She was in a foul mood.

"Good news I hope."

A chill ran through him, so he was glad for the fire that burnt inside the tavern. The tables had been given a new lick of paint and looked marginally better than before. Eris waved and pointed to tankards of ale he had already prepared on the bar. It was mid light, so the place was almost empty. Only a few patrons at the back muttering about the new rumours that Jefferson wanted to control all User's. Lusha had said they were true on his latest visit.

They moved to the middle table and sipped their drinks. Livia's mood dropped even further but he had little advice left to give. "Maybe it might be time to look for another position so you can move on. This isn't making you happy, Liv."

"He just needs to understand age doesn't matter." It was the same conversation that had occurred all season.

A good hour passed before the door opened again and Relda trailed in. Kreg and then Becca in her wake.

He nearly choked on the liquid he was about to swallow.

Becca's hair was shorter, cut in a bob to her ears, she was thinner and the turquoise had been replaced by a vibrant purple gown…but it was her. In the flesh. So many moon turns had been spent praying for this moment.

He moved towards her, deserting Livia at the table and took her in. "I didn't think you…"

"I said I'd try my best. Your beard is bushier. I like it."

"Your hair is shorter. It suits you."

Kreg nominated himself to fetch drinks for everyone, as Esmerelda chatted happily to Liv.

Ivloch just stared at Becca and tried to work out what to do or say. A quarter of a year since Ma had passed and she had last been here. An agonising wait. She had kissed him and said she couldn't share her secrets. Every night he had wondered what they were.

"I missed you, Becca."

Kreg was there, at his side, drinks in hand.

"Sorry to interrupt…erm, 'Relda wants to talk to us all. You all. I'm with her. Is it warm in here?"

They moved to the table. Liv and Becca introduced themselves warmly and he believed the two might become firm friends. It was the first time they had ever spoken, after avoiding each other at the funeral.

"So, we want to share something with you!" Esmerelda sounded incredibly proud and Kreg looked at her in awe. "I can officially announce that we, me and Kreg, the Leshi family, are going to have a baby!"

He had guessed that would be the announcement, but the foresight didn't overshadow the overwhelming happiness he felt as he hugged his two closest friends tightly.

"We saw the Healer this morning but…" Relda continued, changing her voice to a whisper, "…my power. It's a girl. I can feel it! Kreg thinks that's terrifying, but you know, I always wanted a girl." Their happiness was infectious. Even Becca seemed to feel it and she had been oddly quiet during the proclamation.

"Me a dad?! Me, Ivloch!"

He happened to think Kreg would make an excellent father and told him so.

Becca went to work, Eris delighted to have her back. Liv dismissed herself early claiming tiredness but whispered good luck as she passed. He thought he might need it.

Kreg was getting mercifully drunk and telling every patron that entered the building the good news. Most congratulated him by buying him a drink which turned the problem into a vicious circle.

Relda came to dwell next to him, a hand wrapped around her red curls. "I'm still going to join The Guild Ivloch. I want to do good in this world and I want my daughter to see me accomplish it." Her gaze was unusually icy, such ferocity in those blue eyes, but it mellowed as she spoke of the child that he could already tell she adored.

"It'll be a dangerous life for a little one, 'Rel. If what Lusha says is true, then no User is going to have an easy time of it. You could be putting you both in danger."

She nodded and sipped her tonic. Becca's creation; meant to be good for the infant. "I've thought of that; but what if she's like me? It's rarer now, I know, but my bloodline…it's always been strong. I think there's a chance as much as Kreg wants to pretend otherwise. I know what I'm getting myself in for. If she is, she will be safest with The Guild. Even if anything happens to me then they will take care of her…If it did out here, then who would she have?"

"She'll always have me. I promise you."

"I wouldn't doubt it, Youchnore. I'm going to take him home." She pointed at Kreg, a look of utmost love on her pretty face. She hugged him tight and waved towards Becca at the other end of the bar. "You…stay and talk to her when she's done. I know how much you've missed her, and I know there are things she won't tell you, but you should try. For your sake and hers."

"I will. I love you Rel and I'm so damned happy for you." He couldn't help but wonder, if perhaps, Becca had been able to share her secrets with Esmerelda. The notion made him feel quite nauseous.

"We love you, Ivloch. All three of us," 'Relda called.

Kreg managed to fall into the door as she tugged him towards home and he waved lovingly at Ivloch.

Their baby would be a lucky one to grow up with such parents. Wielder or not.

Eight

He waited outside for Becca to lock up and finish. She pulled a smoke from her borrowed fur cloak as she saw him.

"Nasty habit I've picked up," she commented, a fire lighter appearing in her hand. He didn't mind, Liv smoked around him all the time. He often found it relaxing himself, after one too many ales. "What are you doing here?"

"I'm going to walk you home."

"I don't live in Rightwy. I live out towards Wylow. It takes me over an hour to get there. You don't…"

"I want to, and--" he pointed to the blade across his back--"I have this in case a demon catches me on my return. It's been too many moons and I want to talk."

She finally relented and they moved towards the gates. "The red forest is the quickest way." She indicated east and the unique red blooming trees that could only be found in this part of Brodanna. That they knew of. Perhaps over Death's sea lived all kinds of things he couldn't even imagine.

Silence prevailed as they left Rightwy in the distance and began their quest through the woodland. The moon's light mixed with the mass of red to create a tinted glow, which dominated as far as he could see.

"I always think I'm in some kind of fantasy world here, I guess compared to the life our ancients had, we are." Becca was giggling, touching the red blossoms. "It's nice to have company."

The trek was long, branch after branch attempting to attack one of them, fallen trunks in the way of their legs. Becca seemed to shiver, so he put his cloak over her small shoulders. He was aware they had travelled quite a distance and he hadn't said anything he wanted to say. Broaching all the things that had crossed his mind since they parted was a lot harder than he had anticipated. But, it needed to be done.

The awkwardness was starting to make him stutter, but what if he was wrong? What if her parting words had meant little to her?

It was Becca who managed to bridge the void.

"I'm sorry I couldn't come back sooner…there was something really important I had to do. I'm so happy about your apprenticeship though." He looked at her quizzically. He had no chance to mention it. "I went to see Esmerelda as soon as I got back this morning. She told me…about everything that happened, whilst I was away."

"Oh." Had she told her how much he missed her? She had gone to see 'Relda and not him.

"I'm really proud of you and happy for her and Kreg."

"They're going to adore that little girl."

"They are." There was a touch of sadness in her voice. She looked up and noticed his watchful eye. "I'm sorry. They will. It's just a dangerous world and I worry. I've always said I'll never have children. Not whilst Brodanna is like this. It's a personal thing, but they're going to make great parents."

He could understand the concern and felt it himself. The venom from some as they discussed Users, words the King uttered…Brodanna was changing.

"It's why I want to join the King's Men. I thought I would be like Herman but…I might be able to make a difference out there. Protect some people."

"You what? You can't be serious!"

Becca started walking away, faster than he had ever seen her move. The forest stood no chance against her fury.

He bumbled after her, his brain in overdrive. He knew her reaction to Lusha, but could she really think that little of him? To believe that he would turn out like his cousin? Or share his opinions?

He loved Esmerelda… Being a Wielder didn't make anyone any different from him.

If he was part of the fight, then perhaps he could protect them. Make a difference.

"Becca, wait. Please!" He knew he was yelling, but saw little other choice.. She stopped but didn't face him. "You've been gone for four moon turns, and now you're storming away already. Just talk to me. Whatever it is. Talk to me." He could hear the pleading in his voice but wouldn't let himself feel shame. He needed her to listen. "I missed you so much. Every moon. Friends or more, I missed you."

"Do you have any idea what those people do? You listen to Lusha and talk at the tavern, but it is so much worse. You have no idea!" She hadn't turned. Hadn't reacted to him coming towards her.

"Then tell me." He reached for her arm, but she recoiled, whipping round and hitting him with his own cloak.

"They're going to ban them. Hunt them down and lock them away for their own gain. Jefferson doesn't hate Wielders, Ivloch, he wants to them to be his army, just as he is controlling you and everyone else so he can do what he wants!"

"How could you possibly know that?" She had to be mistaken.

She pulled at the cloak and reached her sleeve. The sleeves that were always there. Never once had Becca Jenns not wore long garments which covered the entirety of her arms.

"This is how I know, Ivloch!" She tugged the material upwards and flourished her wrist in his direction. There was a Mark, one that had been burnt on to her porcelain skin. A Mark he recognised but wasn't supposed to; it wasn't meant to be seen in Brodanna. Banned by Jefferson. Anyone who wore it was considered a member of Kara's Guild, an ally of the Black Lands, and an enemy to the throne. To Brodanna.

"Becca…who the hell is he?"

The voice made him whip round. He didn't reach for his blade like Herman had taught him. He just stared open mouthed, as two people appeared from the trees.

The man was round, dark-skinned and barrel-chested with brown hair cut to the scalp, a ring of knives across his calf. The woman wore a fur gilet and a swirling tattoo of thorns across the right side of her face. Her hair was pitch-black, and a thick line of kohl streamed across her eyes.

She pointed a bow in his direction and the man looked angrily towards Becca.

Becca stepped in front of him, her arms wide. "Damonn, Eshaa. Stop. I can explain."

***

Damonn prowled towards Becca as Eshaa didn't relax her aim.

"We don't have time for explanations, Bec. We're looking for you. Something's happened." His accent was strong, with a twang Ivloch had never heard.

Becca was with The Guild. These people must be too.

"What is it?" Becca's voice seemed to change, as if she turned into this 'Bec' he didn't know.

"Your brother and Eshaa went scouting. They found a camp of King's Men and their User puppets. They heard something they shouldn't and tried to report back. They didn't realise they were being followed." Becca let out a weak cry and Eshaa a grunt of disapproval. She clearly didn't like what this man had to say. "They attacked the house and Edwyn…"

"No. No. Tell me he isn't…" Becca was crying. He couldn't see her face, but he could hear the familiar sound. The last few moon turns had definitely lent him to understanding tears and pain.

"He hasn't passed on to Kara yet, but I fear it will happen. The wound is grave and you know he was weak. You have to come."

Becca relocated to Eshaa's side, a brief nod of understanding passing between them. She didn't even look back at him.

"What about him?" Damonn eyed him like prey.

"Let him go, Dam. He is a friend and he will keep my secret. I trust him as much as I trust you."

"No. He knows too much. He comes with us."

"We can't take this man. He is large and we don't know him." Ivloch hoped Eshaa always spoke so plainly and hadn't just taken such an intense dislike to him.

Damonn refused to take no for an answer and asked Ivloch if he would come willingly or needed to be bound. Ivloch assured him he would do what he asked. Becca refused to meet his eyes as Damonn urged him on, to join Eshaa at the front of the party.

"Are we still at the house? What did Edwyn hear? What happened to him? How did we survive? Why did you even let him out when he hasn't been well?" Becca seemed to be full of questions and no patience for an answer.

"He is never not unwell, Bec." Ivloch listened to Damonn speak, it was without any nastiness, only honesty. He had the feeling Becca hated that. "He convinced Esh it would be alright, and I probably would have done the same if I'd been there. He was going stir crazy. We're still at the house. Only three of them came. No Users. I dispatched two. Eshaa one. You'll see what's happened when you get there. It'll do no good to worry more now."

Becca howled and her footfalls became heavier, but faster. He wanted to look back at her, but didn't dare for fear of her ignoring him, or Eshaa's suspicious glare.

"I couldn't worry more if I tried. The news. What did you overhear? What was so important, Damonn? Eshaa?"

"The Queen. She is pregnant again. Six months they believe. They discussed it freely, but news is not meant to have left the palace. With only one heir Jefferson's hold on the throne wasn't secure. A second child spells no good things for our people." Damonn seemed to quicken his pace, as comfortable as he was with the truth, he seemed less so with an angry Becca.

"Can this ruddy day get any worse?" Eshaa's tone matched her scowl. Perhaps she really was just slightly unpleasant.

"My brother might be dying…a Guardian might die, because the Queen got laid? Tell me you're joking."

"The Guild don't know. It's important."

He heard Becca unleash a long string of curses he didn't know she was capable of.

The word Guardian floated in his mind. He tried to remember knowledge of The Guild and why it was important, but it wouldn't unearth itself. If Esmerelda were here… she would also be putting the baby in danger and that was the last thing he would want.

He was quite glad that Damonn hadn't seen fit to remove the blade at his back. It was about the only comforting thing he had left.

They trudged on for what felt like hours. He didn't mind the journey too much, it was the huffing and impatience from Becca that riled him. He wanted not to care, to hate her for not telling him and being this Bec, but he couldn't bring himself to. It was the anguish of the woman he had missed so deeply, and every cry seemed to send a new stab of pain through him.

"We are nearly here. Do we let it walk in?" He could tell Eshaa was talking about him.

"I'm actually not an it. A quite large man as you rudely pointed out earlier…"

"Oh, he does have a tongue. Maybe not such a bad play thing you have here, Bec," Eshaa grinned. A terrifying sight. It seemed to encompass her whole face. He could imagine the look going down well at a dinner table.

Becca cursed again and charged past, moving through the thicker, tighter line of red trees. Almost as if they had been placed there by something other than nature. Damonn sighed and urged him to follow. Eshaa seemed to just chuckle and finally return her bow to its rightful home on her furred back.

A clearing lay beyond where Becca had gone. She was already out of sight. A wooden hut, larger than any in Rightwy, stretched across a wide circle which the trees had left abandoned, a tiny stone path leading to its entrance. Red and green grass mixed across the floor, highlighted in the moonlight. Ivloch had forgotten how beautiful and unique this forest could be when you stopped to pay attention.

A black-haired woman cradling a baby stood at the door, a desolate look spread across her tight face. As he marched closer, he could see a striking resemblance to Becca, but she was dark where Becca was light. So similar; yet so different.

Damonn danced past him and squeezed her and the child. "Tarsha, I'm sorry it took so long. How is he?" He ruffled the child's hair.

"Fine. Who is he?" She asked as she pointed at Ivloch.

"Ivloch Youchnore. We found him with Becca. I thought it was best to bring him, he heard a lot."

"You're Ivloch? Interesting." Becca's smile tugged at the side of the woman's face. "You better come inside. I'm guessing my sister is going to need to talk to you after she's seen Edwyn."

Tarsha gave the child to Damonn and took Ivloch into an almost empty room. The walls were covered in various maps of Brodanna, some belonging to an era far before his time. A singular wooden stool stood in the corner.

"Sorry, we don't have much here but it seemed like the best place. I'll make you a drink. Ale? We have that. I heard you were a fan."

"You know who I am?"

"My sister tells me things, Ivloch Youchnore, and she's mentioned you, once or seven hundred times."

Nine

Edwyn lay in a small cot in the room she knew he called home. He was under layers of blankets that she had no idea how Tarsha had managed to find; she certainly hadn't seen them before. She stepped closer, willing herself to handle whatever came next.

One way or another she always managed, and she could allow this to be no different.

There was blood across his side, which had stained the outside of the blankets. He had been sickly since he was a child. Two years younger than her and Tarsha, born with a Mark that would decide his destiny and a particularly weak immune system. Their parents had taken them straight to The Guild. Healers had been brought in, even the rare Wielder type, but nobody proved able to understand or cure what afflicted him. Weak bones they called it. Organs that didn't work like her or anyone else's.

The Black Lands had tried to wrap him in cotton wool but as soon as he grew, he rallied against the idea. How was he to be a Guardian and protect the one Marked by Kara, if he couldn't even protect himself?

"Let me live," he had pleaded with the Dark Council's Elders. The Guild was ruled by them back then, the separation of the Black Lands and Kara's Guild a new development. A decision that Edwyn had campaigned for. The greatest accomplishment of her brother's life. They would still work closely together but the Black Lands refused to care for the rest of Brodanna or leave their safe mountain range more than was necessary. The Guild wanted to keep everyone safe; as many Users as far from Jefferson's clutches, as they could manage.

"Dark times are going to come on us all, not just here," Edwyn had exclaimed. "Let The Guild be the light that shines on the rest of our world, the force that will fight what Jefferson wants to do. Like the First Guardian hoped. We can work together and separately, but if what we fear will take place, then the people of Brodanna need hope. Kara was the one who gave us this honour. We cannot sour her memory by not doing all we can..."

She had watched the speech in the Hall of Honour only a few moon turns ago. Each Guild member and Black Lander had voted. They would separate but unite when needed. Edwyn at the helm of The Guild. His Mark and its line would pass to the next leader, whoever he may be. A condition set in stone by the Black Lands. The First Guardian's Mark leading Kara's Guild was an old tradition, but one they wanted confirming, if the deal was to be made. It was something The Guild had considered a good thing. She wasn't so sure anymore...

As she rolled back the blanket and saw the severity of the wounds, she prayed that The Guild would be able to flourish under a new leader. On her worst days, she let herself listen to the voice that whispered the Dark Council had seen this coming, known of Edwyn's health and expected the separation to fail...

The vote had been so close.

"Sister, am I about to disappoint you again?" His voice was weak and distant.

"You only disappoint me when you refuse to wear nice clothes. A wound is to be expected."

"Even if it kills me?"

"Even then." She wanted to give him more and tell him there would be a way to save him, but a life among Wielders, learning their trades and magic, had taught her how awful the world could be. They had learnt early in their childhood not to rely on lies.

They had left the Black Lands a year ago... Edwyn wanted to set up other camps across Brodanna and she had sworn to help, as he had known she would. This and one other were all they had accomplished so far. So much time wasted on politics, travelling back and forth and missions she never wanted to remember. Only the separation had been worth the trip.

She was no fighter, but the undercover work was her specialty. Very few expected the pretty and innocent blonde to be a part of The Guild's hierarchy. Her work had been the reason she was in Rightwy. The horrible reason that Ivloch Youchnore was now in this mess.

Master Hobar Reeves had been a member of The Guild since he was twelve years old.

A veteran that even the Dark Landers still admired and they respected very little that couldn't best them with a blade, or a tongue lashing. He bore no Mark on his arm, like every other Guild Member, instead he had taken the Vow on his thigh. Even then they had known he would be a valuable asset in the field. He had sent word through the network, that he believed a powerful User to be hiding in Rightwy.

Becca had meant to collect information, not befriend her. Ivloch, just a complication she tried so desperately to ignore.

Becca Jenns had never been this foolish before.

Edwyn squirmed and brought her attention squarely back to him.

"I'm going to clean your wounds and see what we're working with, and then, we make a plan?"

"Bec…we both know what the plan will have to be. Tarsha and the baby need to be somewhere safe. Across Death's sea will be best. We planned for them to leave next summer anyway." She nodded at him as much as it broke her heart to do so. "You're sure you cannot take my Mark? I think you would be best. You know my dream for The Guild. You can do this."

Edwyn had asked her many times if she would take the mantle if anything ever befell him. Tears threatened to come, but she refused to let them. She faced things as they were. Her whole life had been centred on what was best for Brodanna, for keeping people safe, preventing what could come to destroy them all… It couldn't stop now. Even for her brother...

"I'm a bad choice and you know that logically. I can't fight and I'm not strong enough. Actual Guild members would follow me out of tradition and loyalty to you, but Black Landers would rebel against it. They enjoy tradition but power is their currency. A warrior must be able to stand alone, or no army can be at their back." They were old words. Important words. "They cemented the decision about The Guild's leadership; it would put all of your work at risk, if not more."

They had only respected Edwyn because he had learnt to stand when everyone swore, he would not. He had fought in battles and vanquished enemies when nobody believed he would live. It had taken all twenty-five years of his life to win them round.

Edwyn sighed in defeat. He knew, had always known. Her brother was possibly the smartest man that had ever set foot on Brodannan soil.

She had tried to be a warrior once, but lacked the coordination. Her mind preferred to be behind the scenes, tactics coming far more naturally. There were other ways to be strong than just brute force.

"We must leave soon. Start the journey to the Black Lands. If I don't pass it on to someone you know what that would mean…" Trouble and a power vacuum. The Mark could go anywhere in Brodanna. They would waste more time hunting and arguing while the world suffered.

"Damonn is strong." It was her only suggestion that wouldn't involve her singlehandedly trying to get him south. One she knew she shouldn't make; it went against so many other plans…

"He is a Black Lander, Bec. He may be vowed and blessed with Tarsha, but the blood runs black. It wouldn't be safe for her or the baby either." Edwyn began to cough, a laboured wheezy sound she hated. Blood splattered from his mouth. "I didn't expect dying to be quite this messy. Foolish really. We must go at first light. Clean me. Tonic me. Keep me alive until we get there, please, Bec. One last gift."

"I'll make tonic for the journey and prepare after we clean the wounds." She clutched his hand and squeezed.

"Thank you. One other thing. Fendir. He is at the other outpost. I… help me write a note. Tarsha and Damonn can deliver it on their way. He deserves to know I am to leave him."

She had thought the shattering of her heart complete, but it ruptured further. Fendir Floorson had been Edwyn's true happiness in life. The man he wanted to share every moon, meal or bed with. She doubted she had ever seen two people so in love; except perhaps, for Esmerelda and Kreg. He would not even get a chance to kiss Fendir goodbye or have his love hold him one last time.

She wasn't sure they would make it to the Black Lands, let alone to where Fendir garrisoned some of their other men. There was no way.

"I will see it's done Edwyn. I'll make a vow, if you need me to..." It was a poor joke, one made against Kara's Guild's sacred words, but it caused her brother to release a weak smile.

"Be careful sister. It's our vows that get us in all this trouble, remember."

He coughed again as she left the room.

***

Edwyn's wound ran deeper than she thought. An infection spread through his blood, but she did what she could and bandaged him as she was taught. The tonic would have to do the rest.

There was no time to speak to Ivloch privately as she grabbed ingredients, and various pots and assembled everyone in the room Tarsha had left him in.

Damonn put baby Toba to bed and collected Eshaa. Tarsha had already been there, deep in conversation about Darkstars with Ivloch. She heard him claim he had never seen one and Tarsha enveloped him with a description of their leathery wings and snapping teeth. It would have made her smile on a different moon. So many times, she had envisioned introducing him to her family; involving him in her life.

It had been a rather irresponsible fantasy.

She stretched out her ingredients on the floor and directed Tarsha to two of the pots. "The tonic of Bliss. We must make enough to keep him alive for...however long we can, or the journey will be a waste." She didn't have to explain what journey, Tarsha had clearly grasped the next step. She always did. Becca couldn't miss the grimace that crossed her face. The way her cheeks would pull in, shock in her eyes. She imagined it mirrored her own.

"It will not stop the pain, Bec."

"I know, but anything that does may weaken the senses, and we need him. We need him to be alive. That's what matters." Her next words tore a part of her soul away that Becca wasn't sure she would ever get back. "This is more important than his life. We all know that."

Eshaa lent down to help Tarsha. "He is strong and he will get there. I believe it and so should you. Has he not fought at every opportunity for his survival? I will come with you. I like the man who defied our law. I will help." Becca nodded gratefully and hoped the girl was genuine. Eshaa's blood certainly did run black.

Now would come the harder part. She let herself sneak a look towards Ivloch. His blonde hair was tussled and the beard stuck out even more than usual. So much fuller than when she had left Rightwy after Sara Youchnore's death. It made her want to go and hold him. He was such a big man, but so gentle, although twice as deadly if Master Reeves was to be believed. He had sung his praises in all the meetings she had with him.

"The boy, the boy, may be better than even Herman, you know? Four times as nice. He is big, like a tree, but he moves fast for the size. I would not want to fight the boy, even at my best." The old man loved him. He let few into his heart, but those he did, stayed with a ferocious adoration.

"Ivloch, you should go. Can you find your way back?" She wished she could say more but there was not time and not in front of The Guild. Would he go back to Livia? She hadn't dared ask if what had passed between them had continued. She thought he had been happy to see her, but he had been with the woman. She should be happy for him if it had. It was a much better match; one that might see him happy.

"No." It was Tarsha, before Ivloch could speak. Her ingredients passed quickly on to Eshaa. "He looks like he knows what he can do with that blade. I know where you're going to send me, Damonn and Toba. That means it will just be you and Eshaa getting Edwyn to the Black Lands. There is no time for anyone else or us to send word. You'll need him."

Her sister moved to the man Becca cared for and bowed at his feet. Ivloch looked flabbergasted and horribly uncomfortable; he had no idea what he should do. Almost another reason to laugh.

"Ivloch Youchnore, I don't want to go away, but I know I must for my son's sake. It will be dangerous without my brother and I can't risk his life but…I know you care for Becca, and she for you. Please see her and Edwyn safely reach their destination."

A silence fell across the room. Becca even stopped frantically mixing her tonic. All eyes on Ivloch. What would he be thinking? Would he hate her for not telling him any of this? For what she was involved in? Or would he understand?

He reached out a hand to Tarsha and stood, pulling her up with him.

"I'll see them safely there. I promise." Oh Ivloch, don't make promises you can't keep, she wanted to say, but she kept her lips tightly closed. A person must be responsible for their own words; their own actions.

"He is not Guild or Black Land. Some will not like it. The Black Lands don't allow outsiders. You know this and our times." Eshaa had no tone of malice, just fact. It was the Black Lander way and had to be honoured.

"He isn't doing it for either. He is doing it for me, and my brother, and we will vouch for his safety." Becca knew she sounded more confident than she felt, but Eshaa assented without protest. That meant she would do all in her power to make sure Ivloch Youchnore would help them and survive the experience.

***

The tonics were bubbling. They would need several hours before they were ready to help Edwyn. She had sent Eshaa out with Ivloch to show him how Edwyn's cart worked. They had previously used it when the bones inside him had betrayed him on long journeys, and luckily brought it here.

She indicated that Damonn should shut the wooden door behind him. They were alone and discussions had to be had. The ones they hadn't wanted

Eshaa to know. Even Ivloch and certainly not Edwyn. He needed to think he had at least got his nephew to safety.

"Are the arrangements complete?" Becca asked. Tarsha seemed angry. She had never wanted this.

"I have a house set up, the other side of Wylow. In the forest. Nobody can track it to The Guild or our names." Damonn was as efficient as always. His loyalty may have begun with the Black Lands, but he prioritised the vow he had taken with Tarsha and the son they created together.

It was something set in motion for moon turns. Crossing Death's sea might bring them to safety, but nobody knew what awaited on the other side. It was dangerous for a child so young. The Guild's vow was meant to be for life, held above all else unless extreme circumstances allowed some leeway. It had been Becca who decided this situation fit. Fendir, who had helped her. Edwyn believed they would go across the sea. He had to. If The Guild's leader was ever discovered to have released them...

"Fendir will have documents for you. New names. All three of you." Tarsha had loved the name Toba and chosen it carefully. "Tarsha, you will have to burn away your Guild Mark. There is no other way. You hide there. Become farmers, do whatever you must. I'll contact you when I can, and it's safe, but that's all. Don't approach me, The Guild, or any Black Lander. Do I make myself clear?"

They agreed, despite every part of her sister rallying not to.

"You live your lives and you be happy. No getting involved with any Wielders or saving anyone."

Becca hoped the separation would not be forever. Tarsha was the best part of her. She would find her sister when time allowed, hopefully see Toba grow up and turn into a brilliant young man. One moon they might be able to help The Guild again, but it could not be now.

"You take care of her, Damonn. Toba too. Keep them safe. You tell no one. Fendir will keep his word and do the same."

"I have vowed it to you. I will not break that."

She could only pray to Kara that was the case.

Ten

He managed only an hour of sleep before light found its way through the wooden panels of the house.

Becca still hadn't spoken to him alone, but he couldn't stop himself feeling for her as he watched her say goodbye to her sister and nephew. Toba didn't seem to understand what was happening, but gurgled happily in his aunt's arms, as her tears fell on his hairless head. Tarsha wept at both Becca and Edwyn.

It was easy to forget that she would never again see her brother.

Eshaa had placed Edwyn on the large cart, wrapped in a variety of blankets, a strange tenderness in the Black Lander's gestures. The man himself was ghostly, thick bandages wrapped around several parts of him.

He was thinner than Ivloch had expected and much shorter. Such prominent cheekbones and arms no thicker than petite Becca's. He had stared at Ivloch openly when he first saw him, a reluctant and pained grin on his face.

"I hear you are to be my new protector. I'd like to shake your hand and say thank you, but it appears I'm a little indisposed." A laugh and a cough erupted from his cracked white lips. "I do appreciate what you are about to do, Mr. Youchnore, for me, The Guild and my sister."

Ivloch thought he liked the man. He could see why, despite the ailments Tarsha had warned him of, even before such an injury, people had followed him. It tickled him to think of the way Kreg would react to such a man… the fear, the jokes and the wish for a drink.

Would Kreg or Esmerelda have noticed he was gone yet? He imagined them still tucked up in bed, thinking of the child they were about to have. He hoped that's what they were doing.

"We will make sure Fendir gets your letter, brother," Tarsha was declaring, and kissing the injured man's head. Edwyn seemed to tense even further at her words, the only sign of weakness he had allowed to be prevalent. It made Ivloch wonder who Fendir was.

Tarsha hugged him, something which made him feel horribly awkward. He placed his arm rather unsteadily round her. 'Relda was the only one who usually showed such emotion. It wasn't that he hated it, only that he was never sure how to respond.

"Take care of them. I beg you," she pleaded.

"I'll do what I can." Becca avoided them, fussing with Edwyn and making sure the tonics were packed safely.

"We should go. Time will run out and we will all be in the shit." Eshaa had been impatient since everyone first awoke. Already dressed in more fur than he thought could fit on a person, with weapons hanging off every place one possibly could. She had quite the collection.

They were walking away from the hut before he knew it. A path led from the back of the house which had clearly been cut down for Edwyn's cart. He wondered if it had been Eshaa, or Damonn who did the deed. The unusual mix of grass colours, trodden underfoot by wheels and people, caught his eye. So beautiful in the light.

Eshaa pulled the cart, refusing to allow either him, or Becca a chance. "This is my turn to be useful and do my part. You two…do whatever it is you need to do."

That turned out to mainly involve walking in an uncomfortable silence and glaring at the scenery. He had anticipated that Becca would be more upset after they left, but a steely resolve seemed to have flooded her. He was torn between utter admiration, and a wish to know her better.

What had she faced out here, all the times she hadn't returned to The Seven Whiskers? What made her believe in The Guild so reverently? If she could handle this, he could only imagine what had come before. He wasn't sure such loyalty could only originate from her brother's relationship with The Guild, or the thing which was on his skin.

Edwyn seemed deathly silent as they trundled on. Still so much forest to clear before they could go south.

The Guardian comment had ruffled him. Tarsha had bristled into the room last night, when he hadn't been able to sleep, and explained.

Kara's spell had meant five Guardians were created, all to protect and honour the one that would bear her own Mark, and part of her own power. The person that may have a chance to stop The Unforgiven from returning and destroying Brodanna. There was something about a sword and a crown being crucial too, but Tarsha had refused to tell him everything.

"You aren't part of The Guild or Kara's way, I can't break my vow and tell you it all, but you need to know why Edwyn is important. It's his Mark that will now lead The Guild. The only one the Black Landers will respect or honour and that shit means a lot to them."

He thought he was starting to grasp it; how important these Guardians were and Kara's chosen. Tarsha hadn't answered any questions about whether she had met the one Edwyn was sworn to protect.

"You can take care of someone and what they mean in many ways. Edwyn was never a true warrior, he handled himself at points…but, he has done more for Kara's Marked in these times than anyone else, and that needs to be known and continued. I won't give you a name for Jefferson's men to torture from you. I owe that to him. There would be nothing he wants more than to control The Guild."

There was so much they weren't telling him; the good and the bad. In some ways it was a relief. He could focus on the task ahead, and that's what he preferred to do in all things. Curiosity, however, was a dangerous animal, one he had been befriending for too long, and the resolution being so close was all too tempting.

Becca sneezed and he thought about the irony of where his thoughts had been. "I hope you know I'm sorry." Her attention stayed on Edwyn and Eshaa, but he was sure the sentiment had been meant for him.

"Why were you there? What does Rightwy have to do with any of this?"

She told him then. Master Reeves had settled there in his old age but still worked religiously for The Guild; passing them information or finding new recruits.

Lusha Youchnore's bragging had helped provide him with intel they otherwise wouldn't have received. Reeves had known about Esmerelda. Becca had been there to recruit her.

He could feel his mouth go dry and the hairs on the back of his neck stand to attention. Two of the closest people to him had lied; how could Reeves and Becca have done such a thing? 'Relda had been in danger...

"Her powers are much stronger than she knows Ivloch. Her line goes back generations, one of the only families to always produce a Powered baby. She could be a valuable asset, we need support, especially Users."

"Was your friendship with 'Relda a lie? Kreg? Just a game to get her to work for you?" He left off the 'what about me?' that he wanted to ask. Her swift glance in his direction told him she knew.

"It was meant to be. I guess I'm not quite as good at undercover work as I hoped. I ended up caring about all of you, and I intend to make sure the Leshi's are protected."

"You know Esmerelda will join you if you give her the chance. The baby..."

"The baby will inherit her power. If it's a girl as she claims, and that family has always had certain foresight, it will be hunted across Brodanna, murdered or shoved into one of the camps Jefferson is planning. They will find her eventually. Death will be the kinder option if what we believe Jefferson's intentions are, come to fruition. The Guild will protect her."

"Becca, you can't know that!" What could she possibly be thinking...? He remembered Esmerelda's last words to him. The fact Becca had gone straight to see her. "She knows. About you. You told 'Relda everything."

"Yes. I did. I offered her a place in The Guild and I intend to honour the proposition. I know what this world is like. I'd rather that child grew up to be an ally of The Guild and use her immense power to aid other Wielders, than be turned into a weapon to be used against us." She pursed her lips and turned those green eyes on him.

"The Unforgiven are gone. They're practically imprisoned spirits, if they even still survive. What about Kreg? That baby-" He was furious, how dare she think of 'Relda as a game.

"You have so much to learn, Ivloch Youchnore."

"…And you need to learn to care about people Becca Jenns!"

*****

It took hours to get through the forest, and Becca insisted they stop only to give Edwyn more tonic. He slept when the pain allowed. Ivloch was impressed he never cried out or asked for anything the whole way. He seemed like a braver man than he himself, would have been in such a situation.

The forest had given away to more fields and the occasional small town or homestead, which Eshaa insisted they avoid at all costs. Two men on horses passed them on the road and warned that the miles ahead had very soft ground. Eshaa seemed suspicious of them, but Becca insisted they were just simple travellers.

The spiralling market town of Starla caused the most trouble. They had to go around it and that added an entire moons travel.

"Too many risks. The King's Men are always there." The first words Becca said to him since their argument.

Ivloch got to look from a distance. Starla looked wonderful. Coloured walls surrounded it, blues and greens and purples. It was three times the size of Rightwy and the only other place he had ever seen, bar Wylow. Kreg and 'Relda would know he was missing by now, but he doubted they would ever believe he was seeing such things.

As they swerved to avoid the town, Eshaa started to tire so he took over with the cart. She was furious at her own weakness and made Becca vow to tell not a soul that exhaustion had beaten her. Becca looked amused but agreed. "Whatever you say Eshaa."

Edwyn spoke to him as he pushed. He told him stories of the Black Lands and the first time he ever saw a Darkstar fly. "They say when Brodanna was created they flew all over. Can you imagine?"

Ivloch could and didn't know if the idea excited or terrified him. Much like the journey. "Do they always stay in the Black Lands now?"

"Not always, but they stay close to home unless they have claimed a rider. They prefer to only range further with a companion on their back. Odd for such creatures; but all the more beautiful."

Ivloch couldn't help but agree.

Edwyn also spoke passionately of The Guild and what it was like to carry the Guardian Mark. "When I was a boy, I thought they had it wrong. Me, so weak and fragile, protecting someone? It seemed like a cruel joke of nature, but a man can do a lot when he is determined, Ivloch Youchnore. I would have had my life no other way."

He heard Becca release the smallest of sobs as Edwyn unleashed the confession.

"What was that?" Edwyn asked, his own laboured breathing making it difficult for him to hear.

Ivloch turned back, but Becca was frantically shaking her head. The message seemed clear; *don't let him know how much this is hurting me.* He wanted to be mad about earlier, but he wished Edwyn no pain and the logical part of his brain had started to agree with her argument. Not about The Unforgiven. He would need to hear more, but about Esmerelda and Kreg's daughter. If 'Relda was as powerful as Becca, and apparently Reeves believed, then she would need all the protection she could get. Little Kreg had no idea what he had got himself in for, but Ivloch doubted he would have had his life any other way either, if the choice had been offered.

"Just my throat being odd I think, Edwyn. Nothing to worry about," he lied and considered Edwyn far too smart not to realise.

"What do you want to do with your life, Ivloch Youchnore?" The cough that ran through his body seemed stronger and Ivloch could see the blood which splattered on to his blanket.

It was a big question to answer. Harder still, when asked by a dying man.

"I think I want to be happy, Edwyn. I'm not quite sure how that looks yet, but I'd like to find out."

"That's probably the best answer a man can give to such a question. Certainly, the wisest. I can see why good old Reeves liked you." Edwyn let out a noise halfway between a chuckle and a croak. "I've been happy, that's more than most get."

"That it is. It makes you a lucky man."

"Oh, the luckiest. My partner, Fendir. Best thing to ever happen to me. He… is twice the size of me, always with a weapon, and a bad joke ready for a new moon. He makes me smile even on the worst of days. I think my life would have been very different if I hadn't known him."

Edwyn seemed to fall into a sleep as soon as he stopped talking. The man had somehow got paler; an achievement, considering how he had looked that morning.

It seemed like one of the cruellest twists of fate that this man wouldn't get to say goodbye to the one he loved so desperately. A punishment Ivloch couldn't even begin to imagine.

Eleven

They were finally forced to stop for the night.

Starla still sparkled in the distance, but they had found an outcrop of wood that would hide them from the road. Edwyn had grown weaker, his silences longer. Eshaa seemed to nearly be falling on the floor and Becca's face constantly wore a frown. Even Ivloch could feel the muscles in his arms giving way.

He helped Becca pull the bed rolls from the cart whilst Eshaa cooked up some clorix meat she had salted and brought with them. A wicked grin, as the tiny fire she made, reflected in her brown eyes. They ate in tired silence, Becca spoon feeding Edwyn. He managed three mouthfuls before slightly shaking his head and murmuring for no more.

Becca failed to hide her worry.

"I'll make it sister. Just tonic me."

Becca insisted on taking first watch. "You will both decide on pushing the cart tomorrow. If we move fast, we may make it in a day, you'll need to rest."

Both he and Eshaa tried to argue but knew it was in vain. Her logic always won out.

Ivloch also got the impression she wanted to avoid him. They still hadn't spoken personally since the argument. He wanted to ask more questions but didn't know if he could trust himself, or Becca, to keep their temper.

Eshaa fell asleep as soon as her body hit the floor. Ivloch tried but failed.

He was glad he was awake when he heard Edwyn call out. He moved to aid him and Edwyn seemed to indicate the wounds along his side. Ivloch lifted up the blankets tentatively, afraid of what he was about to see and wishing Becca was there, whilst understanding Edwyn had waited until exactly a time she wasn't.

The bandages were coated entirely in dark blood, a green pus oozing between the wetness.

"My moon's waning has not yet arrived, but it will not be long. I fear we won't make The Black Lands." Edwyn's voice was strained, a pant to each word.

"I could go ahead. There will be a horse in Starla. It will be quicker. If they come to meet us?" It was the only idea he had, and then Eshaa could push the cart...

"You do not know the way, and even if you did, they will not let you in."

"I will go."

Both he and Edwyn moved their heads towards the sound of Eshaa's voice. Ivloch felt like a fool for believing her to be already unconscious. Becca was clearly correct--he did have a lot to learn.

"I will go to Starla, take a horse and ride for home. They will come at my command, and we will meet you. I ride faster and better than most. I will be there by morning if I go now." Ivloch wanted to dispute her plan, to tell her she was tired, and it would never work, but he said nothing. Edwyn had been correct that he didn't know the way; but being of so little use was never a comfortable experience.

"You will not betray me, Eshaa?" Edwyn asked.

The Dark Lander walked towards him and placed her pale and surprisingly uncovered hand on his cheek. "I vow it. I am fair to The Guild and my people and you have won my respect, Guardian Edwyn. Do not die before I bring help."

A raspy chuckle emerged from Edwyn's mouth as he tried to clasp her hand. "Ride well my friend."

Eshaa spared no time for Ivloch, or to inform Becca of the plan as she collected her weapons and ran back in the direction of Starla. He pitied anyone that tried to stop her from stealing a mount.

"She will do what she can. It is Becca I fear for now, even more than me or The Guild. Strange really, when I think of what this land will face. I may well be the lucky one yet again."

As Ivloch stared open-mouthed, down at Edwyn's small broken frame, he couldn't help but think he would use a different word. "We will get your Mark passed on. Could Becca not?... The separation will work for your Guild." He hoped it was true. He knew so little of the subject; yet Edwyn seemed so devoted to his work. For fate to be that cruel-

Edwyn coughed as he explained why Becca could never bear the Guardian Mark that sat on his wrist and abdomen. Ivloch had no idea that the Mark manifested in more than one location.

The Guardian before him found that idea hilarious, and he encouraged him to lift the blankets and look at it in detail. "It is bigger there, clearer. Quite a beautiful image really. If you can stomach looking at my wound then it will be easier to study."

The shield, the sword, a crown and a swirling G. All so detailed, with a singular circle underneath. It was quite the sight.

It surprised him how magnificent he found it. How part of Edwyn it seemed to be.

"Each one has a slight difference. A small way to indicate which line we have received it from." Edwyn ran his lean fingers across the small raised circle at the bottom. "This is mine. From the first Guardian. It is quite the prize." Ivloch wanted to ask what differences the other Guardians had, if Edwyn knew them, but didn't push the issue.

He should force him to rest and preserve whatever energy might be left, although he sensed that was not what Edwyn wanted. Instead Ivloch found the tonic and poured some into his willing mouth.

"You will take care of her when I am gone? Without me or Tarsha, she will have no one."

"If she will let me, then I will do everything I can."

"She will let you. I know my sister. I am quite sad I won't get to see you make one another happy." Ivloch felt himself blush. Edwyn's idea seemed quite unlikely. "You will face The Guild and our enemies for her?"

It was a strange question. One he hadn't seen coming, or, considered an answer for. This was new to him, all of it, and Becca would barely even speak to him, let alone want him by her side, as she faced the adversary she feared so badly.

Then he remembered Master Reeves and 'Relda, Kreg, the baby and Livia. Even Ma. How he would follow them across Death's sea if they asked. He cared for Becca just as much. Even when he had tried to forget the strange woman from the tavern, who had taken so long to even like him. The girl who wasn't what she seemed and kept more secrets than he had ever known. There would be no going back to a normal life in Rightwy after this.

"I will." He meant it and the epiphany seemed to lift a weight from his shoulders. "I wish I had known you better, Edwyn."

"I think I can grasp a person's character quite quickly, Ivloch Youchnore, and I believe you to be one of the good ones."

The compliment embarrassed him. Becca had been so angry because he thought of joining the King's Men. Had he really wanted to go and protect people like Relda, and make a change? Or had it been just an easy option? The simplest way to escape Rightwy; without taking any kind of risk.

This man dying before him had accomplished so much and never ran away from what life, Kara, or The Transmitter had thrown at him. Had made the choice to stand and fight, even when the odds were against him, on more than one occasion. He simply embraced and made the best of a bad situation. Even not being able to say goodbye to the man he loved, or spending his last days trying desperately to save his people…

"I'm going to try and live up to that, Edwyn. I vow it to you, and I'm getting the impression they are quite important."

"Oh, you have no idea." He tried to laugh but shook with a rattling cough.

"Edwyn, can you tell me about The Unforgiven?"

Edwyn obliged him.

"Kara vanquished them as best she could, but even she wasn't powerful enough to destroy them or send them away forever. They joined together, you see, all of The Unforgiven, against the people. They wanted the barrier down, to escape, go home, fight another war…who knows. That much power… It was stronger in the early days of Brodanna. It would be unmatchable now.

"Kara believed she would sacrifice herself, but Brodanna would grow larger. More Wielders to fight them off; a fair fight one day when they finally broke the containment, she placed them in. She wasn't to know that The Seven Worlds cursed this place and everyone who chose to come here. Our power dies out. Less and less children, each season, born with the gift of magic. The Unforgiven still live, not their bodies but their minds, as powerful as ever. They just need hosts to return, and enough power in one place to rip a hole in their cage. If Jefferson starts rounding up Wielders, then he can rip that hole and start bringing them through. If they find a way to bring enough of them…the barrier around Brodanna will fall. It will mean the end of the world as we know it and we have nothing to protect ourselves."

Oh, to the Transmitter.

"It's highly likely The Seven Worlds, if they still exist, would destroy Brodanna and everyone on it. Who knows what else is out there if The Transmitter exists? The Unforgiven would take us, and the ones we love as hosts. Kara's Marked, the Guardians, and the remains of her spell, are our only hope at stopping them. It's why The Guild, working with the Black Lands, Users…it matters so much."

Ivloch had never been so at a loss for words.

"There is more. Much more; but that is all I am allowed to say. Inheriting the First Guardian Mark is more important than most know. I've been troubled with secrets since I was old enough to know what one was, Ivloch Youchnore." Edwyn looked as if he was finally about to give in to tears; but only for a second. "It makes me pity whoever will end up with my Mark, it's a burden I would not want to share with anyone."

"What kind of secrets?" Ivloch thought he might regret asking.

"Things that might change this world one day, when it's ready. In a good or bad way, I am not the man to say. There are always things more important than ones self; things we must protect until our dying day. Things that we will never truly understand, but hopefully, someone will."

Edwyn let out another hacking cough but seemed determined to keep talking. "It is all part of a prophecy; one I have never even told my sister of. The knowledge I carry is only one small piece, and there is no complete version left on this side of the sea, or the other, I fear. No way of putting it all together. Believe me, I have tried. Time or purpose has taken it from us; and it may very well be the key to our safety or destruction."

"Why are you telling me this? If you've never told Becca?"

"Dying loosens a mans tongue, Ivloch. I can only apologise that it's you who must hear my sins, discover the true weight of my destiny, but my time is running out. I have not told you more than a man should know, nor will I, and I hope you do not think badly of me for sharing the pain."

"Never. I think you're a very brave man Mr Jenns. Very brave indeed." He wanted to ask more, if any other part of this prophecy was known, but he could see Edwyn's eyelids finally flickering, exhaustion pulling at the edge of his vision.

He was well aware he didn't truly understand what Edwyn meant; he wasn't even entirely sure that the man himself did, the amount of pain he was in, but he knew it was important. Knowledge that had haunted him, and would haunt the next Guardian. Another task he had attempted; but never been able to complete.

Ivloch had often been called a trusting man. He believed he had a knack for telling when someone meant what they said. It was how he always knew that when Kreg promised not to drink too much, he was lying.

Edwyn had no reason to lie, as preposterous as his story was.

The horrifying look of sorrow painted across his thin features told him everything he needed to know.

Becca's worry about the baby made spine-chilling sense.

She may not know of the extra burden that had sat on her brother's shoulders; but she certainly grasped the seriousness of what was to come.

The Unforgiven that could devastate their world; as they had destroyed one before.

"I'm glad you understand what we face, Ivloch Youchnore. The Guild is going to need people like you."

He let Edwyn finally drift off to sleep, but the insomnia that had plagued him previously, felt like nothing, compared to the stark future he could now envision.

Sleep would not be coming for him this moon. Lusha supported Jefferson. Kreg was scared to help The Guild but had no idea what the alternative meant. 'Relda and that poor baby. The future the child would face...

So much time wasted on resenting Becca for not telling him her secrets, but in reality, she had been trying to protect him from the nightmare that she was fighting. And when she had finally told him...

He hadn't believed her.

Twelve

Watch passed with no interruptions, and she carefully made her way back towards where she hoped they would all be sleeping.

There had been too much time, sat alone in the darkness, to dwell on what would happen to Edwyn, what awaited in the Black Lands and Ivloch's continued presence.

The shadows had a way of unleashing the things you didn't usually allow yourself to feel.

He was turning out to be the biggest accident of her career.

So many undercover assignments in Tonkara, Torlung, the Spykelands, Borden; all successful. All for some giant oaf of a man to ruin it all with that ridiculous smile and the beard he had clearly grown for her.

Ivloch Youchnore had been noticeable as soon as he walked into that decrepit little tavern. His height had taken up the entire doorframe, that unruly blonde hair she liked so much...it would have been impossible not to pay attention. But it had been the kindness he showed the man everyone else avoided, that had intrigued her.

She would be lying to herself if she said his instant interest in her, hadn't also been part of the novelty. It had been a very long time since Becca had been able to focus on intimate things or enjoy the attention of anyone; let alone a man like Ivloch.

She had avoided him until the apology about Lusha's behaviour, despite Master Reeves' insistence that he would be an excellent body to bring to The Guild. He had grown a beard for her. Kept her company as she provided Rightwy's citizens with whatever cold beverage they desired. Shown such kindness to Esmerelda and Kreg. Loved Reeves for the cranky old man that he was.

The morning he had arrived so bedraggled straight from Livia's bed had infuriated her. The mix of worry and sadness about Sara Youchnore's passing and the red-hot poker of jealousy which ate away at her gut.

The stupidity of asking him if he had a good night…

Tarsha had heard the worst of it over the last few moon turns. So many complaints and idle wondering if Reeves was correct and there was a chance that he may join their cause. The hope that he wouldn't; despite the way she felt, or how she missed that stupid crooked smile.

"You'll never know until you ask. Once you talk to this Esmerelda you won't be going back there anyway. Take the chance, sister, for Kara's sake."

"How can I do that to him? You know what this life is. You know what it can mean."

Esmerelda was pregnant, Ivloch was here and nothing ever worked out the way it was supposed to.

It didn't take long for her to realise Ivloch was wide awake and Eshaa was missing. Edwyn rested fitfully in the cart, thick lines of sweat across his knotted brow.

"Where is she?" Ivloch was sitting on his bed roll, the mass of him far too large for sleeping comfortably on it anyway. The hair was somehow a bigger mess than it had been before she took watch, as if he had dragged his fingers through it in frustration, many a time. He looked worried and timid as he explained that Eshaa had tried to ride ahead on Edwyn's orders. She sighed. It was a terrible plan, with such a small chance at success, but it made more sense than she wanted to admit. Anything was worth trying.

"When did she leave?"

"About an hour ago, I believe. Do you want me to take watch?"

"You haven't slept. It's not doing much good with just one of us anyway." If he was going to pull the cart all that way… probably their only hope to reach Eshaa or The Black Landers in time…

"Edwyn told me about The Unforgiven."

Oh Edwyn, her brother was such a fool.

Ivloch was proud and brave and stupid. He would drag himself into this mess and never leave. She had said things on the past moon by mistake, in anger, at herself and him, but he should never have known the true weight they carried.

"I'm sorry I didn't believe you, Becca. I really am."

"I want you to leave after this. Go back to Rightwy. Join the King's Men if you must, but I don't want you to stay with The Guild." Her heart rallied against her words in every way it could, and she turned her back to the man she wanted to go over and hold. That kiss…that kiss had meant a lot to her.

"I don't think I can do that." He spoke softly and she could hear the movement, the steps as he came closer. She wanted to walk away, to force herself to stop standing in this stupid spot and letting him advance. "I know how much you love Edwyn, and I can only guess what this has done to you, but it's not just about you. You know how much Rel, Kreg, and everyone mean to me."

"It's dangerous, Ivloch." He was right behind her; she could feel the heat of him warming her back.

"From what I heard it's going to be dangerous no matter what. I won't turn my back on the people I love, Becca." He placed his hand on her shoulder blade engulfing the whole of its small frame. "You don't have to do this alone."

She turned slowly, knowing there were tears in her eyes. They had wanted to come for a long time. She was strong, had always had to be and hearing those words meant a lot but they weren't just for Ivloch. They were for Edwyn, the Mark, all the things that had been and would come.

If she had lived differently and could take the burden herself… If she had got Edwyn to Fendir to say goodbye… Or Tarsha were here…

"I'm scared, Ivloch. He is going to die, and I don't know if we can do this without him. The Black Lands can't be trusted… I can't save The Guild on my own."

"You're not going to be alone, Becca. I know it's difficult to believe, but I'm going to do what I can."

Her body felt like it shrunk in his arms. She let him comfort her, stroke her hair and wipe away the tears. Now was not the time for more or questioning the action. Answers could come when the mission ended; if it ended well...

"I don't know if he'll make it, Ivloch, even with Eshaa gone."

"I know. We can only do our best and try. Get a couple of hours rest, you're exhausted, and then we'll go. I'll sit with you and keep watch."

When she woke, she was curled up in his lap and she could vaguely hear the sound of him and Edwyn talking. Edwyn, breathing erratically but explaining how Black Landers took no family name but become known for their own deeds, Ivloch making expressions of amazement.

It was odd to think how different this life could have been, if only it hadn't all occurred at once.

Ivloch had been wrong when he accused her of not caring. She cared too much; it was her biggest weakness, one she so rarely wanted to show.

Becca Jenns allowed herself a sad smile before her fight against the clock began.

She had a horrible feeling it was going to be the one she couldn't win.

Thirteen

Ivloch wasn't sure who was more frustrated with their slow pace; Edwyn or Becca.

Scattered towns meant rougher paths. He had had to push the cart and if they were attacked by even a passing loiterer then they would stand little chance. As they headed further south the terrain became rockier, more hills to waste their time and make the journey harder. The cart barely managed to move over some of the hills and the jolt of pain Edwyn made each time it did rattled Ivloch's very soul.

He couldn't help but stare and attempt to take in everything around him, when the task allowed. Rightwy didn't have these massive elevated areas or the wildlife that seemed to be so rife, as the civilization he knew was left behind.

Edwyn, in hushed breaths, had informed him, they were in fact now in Black Lander territory.

Clorixs ran free, some scared of their party, others inching closer. Tabak Cats prowled in packs. Reeva Birds with their long snouts and bright orange feathers flew above their heads, one nearly emptying its bowels on Becca's head.

He also saw his first Shadewolf. They were huge, named after creatures found back on ancient Earth, and Ivloch had only read about them or heard Esmerelda's ever-changing story about the one she had grown up with. They rarely ventured out of Black Lands territory and the only others known in Brodanna, were said to be used by the King, in Tonkara.

They were huge and wonderful.

The one he saw, was nearly as large as him... It had a stunning mahogany coat and huge yellow eyes which bore into his own. It stood on a hill facing them down and only Edwyn seemed unawed at the sight of it.

"I think I always see that one. I swear it must be some unofficial watchdog for the Lands." He sniffed and Becca administrated more tonic. They were running criminally low.

"Does it ever attack?" The sheer bulk of the animal made Ivloch think it could be quite deadly, despite the lack of danger he inexplicably felt as he took it in. Those glowing orbs looked almost gentle…

"They're big like you, but perhaps just as nice unless provoked." It was the first hint of amusement Becca had released all moon.

Darkness came before any of them were prepared.

Becca urged them on, but even to Ivloch's ears she seemed despondent and unconvinced they would make it. "It's about another twelve hours at this pace to the entrance of the Black Lands. I… the animals will only get worse. A hungry Darkstar that's claimed no human, finding prey?" She shook her beautiful head and Edwyn winced. "The south is the largest part of Brodanna and easily the most perilous."

Ivloch couldn't say he particularly liked the idea of seeing a Darkstar only once; especially to then end up in its stomach and there was no doubt that the flying beasts could easily accomplish such a task. This part, Edwyn had painfully chuckled, they did fly free in, human rider or not. Becca had looked so sad; as if she knew it was the last mirth she would ever see her brother release.

"We should camp." Edwyn seemed resigned. He had spoken for much of the morning, trying to lift everyone's spirits, but as the day passed an angry, almost grief-stricken quiet had overcome him whenever he managed to stay conscious.

"If we camp…" Becca's face fell.

"Then I might die out here in the freezing cold, but you might not. Eshaa has gone for help. She'll stand more chance than us."

Becca continued to press on for what felt like eternity to Ivloch's weary bones, before stopping atop a small mound. Edwyn huffed and muttered complaints Ivloch was quite sure he didn't actually want Becca to hear.

"Over there." She pointed her dirt covered arm towards a small outcrop of trees and a tiny pool of fresh water. The first source of water they had come across since the previous night.

"I remembered Tarsha finding it on a past trip. If we must camp, we may as well do it where we can wash this filth away." Becca had a point.

He pushed Edwyn steadily down the hill and under the cover provided from the trees. The chill in the air was bothering him, so he hated to imagine how Edwyn must be feeling in already such a weakened state. The blankets covering his side were coated in a thick line of blood, as if the stitches that Becca had redone that morning had already failed him. Edwyn shook his head slightly towards Ivloch. *Don't say anything.*

Ivloch hated it but did as he was bid. He removed the cloak from around his big shoulders and lay it over Edwyn and the dark ominous stain.

"You'll need to stay warm."

"I thank you, Youchnore. Always."

Becca produced more tonic, the last of it, and set about making them some food. It would be the final meal they would have on the road. Ivloch washed quickly as she heated the small camp fire. Thick layers of mud and grime refused to budge from his skin. His hair was so streaked with brown; he couldn't help but wonder if the original colour would ever fully return.

He was not a man to particularly care about appearances, unless Becca was involved. It mattered little in the long run, but such a normal thought in such a foreign land, tickled him. It was strange the way your mind always tried to cope with what was happening around you. A way to worry about the ordinary things and not contemplate the danger you were allowing yourself to walk in to.

They ate mostly in silence. Edwyn managed one full mouthful, but nothing more. "More for the both of you, I suppose." He tried to smile but pain contorted his face.

Becca paced and Ivloch rubbed her back. It did little, but she clasped his hand and he saw Edwyn watching, a sorrow in his eyes.

"I'm going to go and clean myself up, see if he will talk to you about how he really is," Becca whispered, the softest of kisses brushing his bushy cheek. He allowed himself to touch where her lips had been as she sauntered away. This was a very odd trip indeed.

"I'm glad she has found you," Edwyn wheezed as Ivloch knelt down beside him.

Ivloch didn't wait for permission as he removed his cloak and untucked the blankets from around Edwyn's delicate body. The blood still oozed out, the thick pus stretching across the entirety of the wound and down his side. Black veins had spread across his whole torso, even under the Mark, rendering it a dull grey colour.

"I think the weapon was laced with something. No stitches are stopping it. I don't believe there will be any way to make it last longer, Ivloch Youchnore, not without the tonic and…"

Ivloch's eyes went wide as Edwyn trailed off and he realised what the man was trying to say.

It seemed to take him great effort as he pulled his right arm from the last of the blanket pile and stared at it. The Guardian Mark glowed with a red light, a throbbing running through it, so strong it was visible even to Ivloch.

"It started around eight hours ago. There is not much time left."

"We can push on. You have twenty-four hours in total. What's happened to the one on your abdomen?"

"Within. Sometimes it is less if one pushes themselves. Something can happen within the time frame or you will fall at the end, but we have no guarantee. It is showing me that my time is running out, as if the other indications were not quite clear enough."

Ivloch let himself curse, a thick string of them that Master Reeves would have been dismayed to hear.

"There must be the right person, Ivloch. I have candidates in mind but any of them could be on a mission for The Guild at present, and you understand the importance of this specific Mark. What I have done with it? What it will do?"

He did and he hated it.

Edwyn was covered up again by the time Becca returned. The water of the spring had managed to cleanse her thoroughly and he wondered what he had done wrong. Bar the torn garments she looked ready for work at The Seven Whiskers, with days of travel and turmoil instantly removed.

Edwyn had made him vow not to mention the Mark to Becca. He wanted to, fought a battle with himself that he should; but Edwyn had begged him and to dishonour a dying man's last wish...

Becca, of all people, would understand what a vow meant to Edwyn.

Her brother fell into another sleep and she sat watching him, her arm resting slightly on Ivloch's leg. "We should go as soon as we see any light. It'll be our only chance."

He just nodded. Would Edwyn last that long? What would happen to the Mark if he didn't? It could mean nothing good for The Guild.

She rested her head on his shoulder and he kissed the yellow of her hair. How it reminded him of the sun shining and good days with Kreg and 'Relda, feeling like he was going to pass the apprenticeship, Becca behind the bar smiling at him… Such beautiful, simple times...

Moons gone by, ones that would never exist for him again. The knowledge of what happened in this world would always linger on his shoulders.

"I think I quite like you, Ivloch Youchnore." The words were soft and meaningful.

"It's quite mutual."

"I don't want you to make me any promises that feel like an obligation. I want to…spend time with you, but I get, it will have its complications." Becca released a long sigh, it tickled the side of his neck. "I'll never be the easy girl with a little cottage and three dull fat children. I don't want to bring a new life into this world until it's better. I've always said that."

Images of Esmerelda stroking the burgeoning life inside her and of Tarsha holding her son played in his mind.

"No obligation Becca, the same to you. I'm not good with people. I used to think I'd like children; but I always ran away from the idea if Ma mentioned it. The occasional day dream, but none I ever truly believed. I think maybe life has a different path for me."

"You're better than you think." Becca stroked his cheek and lent towards him.

The past year had left him dreaming about this so many times. To have this woman feel the same way as he did, for her to reach towards him with that look in her eyes…

A kiss that wasn't a goodbye…

It wasn't the perfect situation, they might not have the right time, but to hold her and know they would face the future together…

Becca howled as an arrow launched from the trees and embedded in her bicep.

Fourteen

He whirled Becca behind him. Arrows kept coming. An unexpected onslaught they had no protection against.

One struck his shin and he let out a roar before pulling it out and tossing it to the grassy floor.

Becca was trying to crawl towards Edwyn, his name hollering from her lips. She should have stayed behind him.

Ivloch attempted to reach for Inferno's Kiss where he had discarded it on the ground, too distracted by Becca, but an arrow hurled towards his outstretched fingers.

"Stop. We are here in peace. Who are you?" Words seemed to be the only weapon he could use without further injury. The only chance without knowing how many assailants surrounded them.

Becca kept crawling, Edwyn still seeming so far away. Why had they sat on the rock such a distance from him? So foolish. If he could distract the attackers, then perhaps Becca could get to him. Protect what he carried...

Shapes started to emerge from the trees. Five of them that he could see. All, thankfully, closer to him, than Edwyn.

"Stay where you ruddy are. Hands up. No sword." A bald man stepped before the others, the rest flanking him. He indicated the smallest one, a woman Ivloch noted, should go to retrieve Inferno's kiss. .

They were all wearing the red and black of the King's Men. Jefferson never sent patrols this far south. The Black Lands were dangerous, the only part of Brodanna threatening open rebellion. This unit shouldn't be here. Of all the threats he and Becca hadn't accounted for, this was no angry villager or Darkstar attack.

Becca made the last of the distance between her and Edwyn before she climbed to her feet and raised her small hands in the air. Ivloch saw her pass a brief look of horror in her brother's direction.

The leader advanced. A bow hung across his back, but steel was in his hand. He poked the weapon towards Ivloch; but he refused to let himself flinch.

"Who are you people? Why are you here?" The voice was thick with a ripe Torlung twang. Scars ran across the top of his head and continued over one eye; the iris distorted with white. He had a nose which had been broken several times and a mouth that seemed to know nothing but cruelty. This wasn't the type of man Ivloch had surmised would be in the King's army. He had envisioned a league of Lusha's; not monsters. Master Reeves would have had a lot to say about such a beast.

"We're travellers. That's all. Taking my sick brother to a healer in Starla." Ivloch had always been terrible with lies; but prayed to The Transmitter this one did its job.

One of the others stepped forward, a thick black helmet concealing their face. A chuckle unleashed from the figure which reverberated on the metal over his face.

He began to prowl; a slow menacing stroll towards Becca. Ivloch's stomach twisted, an unfamiliar anger and rage bubbling towards the surface.

"These are no ruddy travellers. Look at them," the man called, reaching his destination. A hand reached for Becca's hair and yanked. She didn't yelp or attempt a struggle. Her steely green eyes glared at the helmet in defiance and Ivloch felt a tug of love pull at his heart. Becca was a braver creature than he would ever be.

"I'm sure we can think of ways to make them talk." A third voice, the soldier nearest their captain. The remaining one, who hadn't spoken yet, took the slightest of steps back. The smallest hint of reluctance.

"King's Men are fools to travel so far south," Becca was hissing, her attention still devoted to the creature clutching her.

The Captain edged towards Ivloch. He recognised the dance. He was aware their size was on par and was attempting to decide if he could dominate during a fight. He would predict Ivloch's movements to be slow, clunky. They always did. The bulk would have been a worry, but being surrounded by colleagues was egging him on, a confidence running through those veins.

"One person's fool is another's hero. Shouldn't you know that lassy?" The Captain spoke towards Becca whilst he finalised his decision on Ivloch.

Edwyn coughed, Ivloch risked a look back to see blood splatter across the blankets, his cloak… "Both fools and heroes end up dead Captain. An important lesson to remember."

The words were ragged but eloquent. Ivloch took them as his signal to move.

Fifteen

Ivloch moved faster than a man his size should be able.

No time seemed to pass between him reaching forward and punching the Captain and the leap to knock over the woman cradling Inferno's Kiss.

The weapon was in his hands and blood was flying.

The woman pulled a scythe from her belt and came towards him with a growl. Ivloch dodged and parried her attacks whilst pushing her backwards.

She cried out as he plunged the tip of the metal deep into her stomach, as blood sprayed upwards and her life ended.

The Captain was still on the floor, holding his bleeding nose. Orders gurgled from his throat as another soldier charged at Ivloch.

He bellowed as he flipped over the attacker, slicing his arm as he went. The soldier used a knife to slide past his defences and tore at the wound already created by the arrow in his leg.

"Your mistake," Ivloch breathed as his sword found the man's retreating neck and sliced. The strength of such a big man and the quality of the blade saw his body crumple, as the head rolled away.

Red coated every inch of Ivloch's tunic and matted to his formidable beard.

She tried to reach out to Edwyn, at the arrow which sat in his chest, but the helmeted guard pulled her further into his arms. Thick leather against the cotton of her gown. Freezing metal from his helmet resting on the top of her head and thick gloved hands tightening by the second on the cream of her neck. "If you so much as wriggle then I will cut his throat. Do you hear me?"

"I do." She could try and kick him, to use her weight to push back but…

If it didn't work, Edwyn would die.

If this man decided to examine Edwyn or get any closer, then everything would be over.

They had never believed they were travellers, but if either her or Edwyn's Marks were revealed, particularly Edwyn's Guardian one, then who knew what would happen.

She looked back to Ivloch, who was facing off against the Captain and remaining guard. The bald leader had climbed back to his feet, his own longsword ready to strike.

"Attack him," the Captain ordered, but the remaining figure hesitated.

"Or you can go and not die here like the rest of your team. You were never meant to go this far south, were you? You can get out of this. Just run and don't look back." Ivloch sounded like a warrior and Becca was impressed.

Reeves had not been wrong about him. He was a great man and an even worthier ally.

The Captain began to laugh. He didn't for a moment believe that a soldier from his unit would disobey an order, but the sound rung hollow as the figure turned and disappeared into the trees. As if they had never been there.

One less foe to defeat on the field; even if all they could manage to do, was live long enough to find each other, on another.

The Captain attempted to dance around Ivloch. He thought he would tire him out. Becca refused to let herself think of the little rest he had or how long he had pushed Edwyn for.

"You're able with a blade for a traveller. Good enough to have been trained." The Captain's words sent a shiver down her spine and she looked towards the badge on the collar of his uniform.

Ellery stood out in stark white letters. A name she recognised. They were one of the largest families in Torlung, loyal to Jefferson from a city away. Not so loyal to the son they had sent to his army. He would have to find his own glory, the reason he was so far south she imagined.

"Stop!" She screeched, and the masked man's hands were tighter on her throat. Hate radiated from him; the type that consumes you and makes you want to kill. To release your victims as much as yourself. Becca could almost pity such a beast.

The Captain and Ivloch both seemed to pause to look at her. Even Edwyn's hazy eyes tried so desperately to focus.

"Let her talk." The Captain didn't lower his weapon as he spoke but the man behind her eased his grip, just enough for her to bring a voice back to her throat.

"You can go. Both of you. Follow your friend. Nobody has to die here. What happens if you do? You'll have no honour. The Ellery family will write you out of history. You can't want that, or you wouldn't be here." She forced herself to sound stronger than she felt. "You accomplish nothing by dying with your men or even killing us. What prestige do three idiots in the wild accomplish? You have lost too many men. You wouldn't even get our bodies back to Tonkara. Go before it's too late."

The Captain faltered, a small sway forward. Becca decided to take the chance and proceed on.

"You're the youngest brother to Claudius Ellery. You must be. You were attacked by a User and that's why your betrothal was cancelled. The other family hated your scars. I remember hearing about it. Don't let them hear you died here and not care. You still have a chance to live up to your name."

It had started as a guess but she became certain, as his face fell, that she had hit the mark. Tarsha had heard of the story on a mission. The handsome lord, the only thing he had going for him, turned into a nightmare by a terrified Wielder. The family that refused to care and sent him to be the King's offering. Only made Captain because of the surname.

"You know nothing of me!" He roared and whipped his sword through the air as if it was a plaything.

Becca saw Ivloch look between her and him. He was ready if this didn't play out the way she wanted.

"I don't, Garth, but I can. Brodanna can."

He dropped the sword at the sound of his name and began to walk backwards. Slow steps at first and then quicker, the reality of his situation dawning on him.

How wrong he was. He could bring down Kara's Guild if he proceeded. Jefferson would reward him beyond his wildest dreams. She should order Ivloch after him, as awful as the decision might be, just in case-

The masked warrior shoved her to the floor as he grabbed a knife from his belt and flung.

"For ruddy sake. He couldn't do anything right."

The dagger landed perfectly in the neck of the retreating captain. His body fell before Becca could unleash the scream in her throat.

He pulled her back to her feet, another knife brandished at her back. She felt it dig in, a wetness began to trickle.

He snatched her left arm and forced the ripped sleeve upwards.

Oh Kara, how had she not noticed?

The arrow protruding from her arm, had split the cotton, a long line of fabric falling away down to her wrist. The poke of her Guild Mark visible if you paid any attention. He clearly had.

"That fool may not believe a prize is worth taking, but I do. If one of you is Marked, then you all will be." He was pushing her towards Edwyn, towards the cart and her brother's arms hidden under Ivloch's cloak. Towards the wrists which would tell him exactly how much of a prize he had found.

He pushed her head into the cart, a grunt emitting from underneath the helmet. "Who are you, woman?" he hissed.

She felt the weight lift off her before she could muster a response or plan to save Edwyn. The pressure of the awful man disappearing so speedily it seemed as if she almost imagined him. She took a deep breath as her face stopped being buried in the cart. Edwyn retched, spraying blood in her hair. The arrow in his chest-

She turned, terrified of what her eyes would show her.

The man was on the floor, Ivloch's sword surged into where she knew his heart would be. Blood run freely from underneath the jet-black helmet.

Ivloch was staring at her, open-mouthed. The deeds he had just undertaken lowering his shoulders in a way she doubted he could ever recover from. She didn't know if he had ended a life before; it was not a thing to be ignored or forgotten. The weight would change a person.

This was what it really meant to be part of Kara's Guild.

The actions and suffering you would witness for thousands who would never thank you or whisper your name. Parts of your soul destroyed or so rotten they would be of no use again. She had gone through the ordeal herself. The Becca that had existed before…such an odd notion. Ivloch would feel the same someday; she could only plan to be by his side when it came.

"I couldn't let him hurt you." He sounded so small, so vulnerable and she went to him, reaching for his hand to pull him away from what he had just done. What he would inevitably have to do again in the future, if he truly did desire to be involved in this life.

She brought her hands to his moon like face and scrubbed away as much blood as she could. There was nothing to be done about the liquid soaked into his beard until they could get him back to the water.

"I love you, Ivloch Youchnore." She kissed him. Slowly at first and then pushing herself into him, letting him know he too, wouldn't have to face any of this alone. His tongue was cold, lips rough against hers, but she liked it. It wasn't the same as the kiss they had shared in Rightwy. This one felt like a promise.

Never alone, always for each other and Brodanna.

"Together," she whispered, pulling away only slightly. His towering head lowered down to rest on hers.

"You'll be wanting a betrothal vow next, Becca Jenns." He kissed her brow, his arms circling her body, careful to avoid the arrow still sticking out of her arm. The damned thing that had nearly ruined everything.

"One day, Youchnore. One day." He cried and chuckled all at once. Tears which fell into her hair and on to her face. An anguish she knew he had to release. She had done the same after battles or the darker days she daren't remember.

Then she returned her attention to Edwyn and all happiness left in her world evaporated.

Sixteen

The arrow had punctured one of Edwyn's lungs.

They were meant to have hours but would instead be left with minutes.

Becca was kneeling at his side, her hands trying to stop blood from leaking out the fresh wound. It would make no difference and they all knew it.

There were slashes of red on his mouth as he opened it to try and speak.

"The warning, you haven't had the warning…" Becca sobbed, uncontrollable shaking which she no longer seemed to have the energy to attempt to hide from Edwyn.

"He had the warning this afternoon, Becca." Ivloch put his arm around her and ignored the look of fury which shot in his direction, then back towards Edwyn.

"You selfish ruddy shit, Edwyn Jenns! How could you not tell me!" Her body seemed to fall on top of her brother as he used whatever energy he had to extend towards her.

"Heroes and fools, Becca, heroes and fools." More crimson escaped Edwyn's chapped mouth, but he regarded his sister with so much love.

"I'll take the Mark. I'll do my best." She pawed at her eyes, willing the weakness to disappear. She wanted to be Guild member Becca. The one who could handle situations like this and would take that Mark upon her wrist, without questioning what it would mean for her own life. That it might not be enough…

"My darling Becca, you cannot, and you know it." Edwyn whimpered as he struggled to turn his head. "He can though."

It took Ivloch a moment to realise that Edwyn meant him. Becca, a second longer.

She pulled away from Edwyn and rested on her haunches. "He…isn't a Guild member, Edwyn. He doesn't know the ways. He isn't meant to be involved in this mess!"

"Yet he is a formidable fighter and clearly your paramour. You say he has worked for Reeves. Trained under him and Herman. It is not so much of a lie. He was our secret preparation and weapon for The Guild." Another cough ravaged through the remaining life in his body. "Eshaa will find you in a few hours. You will have time to teach him the basics and be at his side in all else. You can get him ready to face them when they come. Sweet talk her. Make her keep the secret."

Becca began to shake her head, she couldn't meet Edwyn's eyes. Her hands were raking through her hair, tugging at her sleeves and hitting the damp earth. "No. Edwyn, you can't do this. There will be another way for The Guild. Not him! Not him!" Her fists kept pummelling as if she wanted to shake the very earth itself, but it would move for no one.

"There is no other way, Becca, and I think it right we ask him how he feels. Don't you?"

He wasn't ready for the pleading look she gave him. They had defeated their enemy, nearly reached the Black Lands, and the woman he loved had decided to love him back.

It had been moons of chaos and wonder.

He was going to stay in this fight already, he knew that, there was no other way to protect the ones he cared for. Staying and leading were very different things. Something he had never prepared for or wanted…

"I am no leader, Edwyn."

There was also the things Edwyn had confided in him; a prophecy and a puzzle he knew so little about. A curse that the man had declared he would want to pass on to no-one.

"Neither was I, but life forces our hand. You have a good heart, Ivloch. You can do the things I've always wanted to do, and you may well be the only chance we have left. I will not force you, the magic will not allow me, but I believe you can do this. Let a man die believing his aspirations can come true."

He could say no. As Edwyn had just said, if he was not willing, he could not make him. He could still serve The Guild at Becca's side and help her in any way he could.

That might also mean watching her fail and her brother's final dream fall to ashes at her feet. It would mean she had to bare the knowledge that had haunted Edwyn's life.

It could mean the deaths of Esmerelda, Kreg and the baby they so desperately wanted.

Tarsha. Eshaa. Reeves. Even Herman or Livia.

There was always a chance to learn.

To be a hero or a fool. On a distant moon he would die either way.

If anyone had to suffer, at least he could do it with eyes wide open. Something he doubted many in Edwyn's line had ever been blessed with. The secret too important.

"I will take your Guardian Mark, Edwyn Jenns. Of my own free will. Until the day I die."

Becca cried out as he walked towards the dying man and presented his right wrist. Edwyn took it with his own, his grip weakening by the second. A faraway look was already in the man's eyes, as if the fight had begun to leave him as soon as Ivloch consented.

"I, Edwyn Jenns, Kara's chosen Guardian, do pass on my Mark to whom I deem ready and fit for the honour. May Ivloch Youchnore be a worthy recipient of this line. May he guard the chosen, love the Guild and always be faithful to those who believe." Blood had fallen from Edwyn's mouth, down his neck and chin. His speech perforated with raspy deep breaths. "Guard, honour and love my friend. I'm glad it's you."

Ivloch's arm began to burn. A tingle in his fingertips first, then waves of heat spreading to the elbow.

He hadn't known of the pain to his chest or the headache which threatened to rip his mind in two. His body fell to the floor, knees deep in the mud, hands clutched in his hair. A wail like none he had ever made emitted from his lips. Every good thing, every bad thing remembered. All the pain of Ma passing, the training, the dad who never returned, his brother's accident in the Spykelands. The euphoria of the apprenticeship, drinks with Kreg, Becca kissing him moments ago, Esmerelda's joyful face as she spoke of the baby, the first time he met Kreg.

A test to see if he was worthy.

Kara's Mark could accept no soul that would not honour their word or deed.

No Guardian could fail the test and live. A warning Edwyn hadn't included; because he believed in him, the pain screamed.

As the agony intensified and all the light before him vanished, Ivloch wasn't sure he would be one of the lucky ones.

A fool indeed.

Seventeen

She cradled Edwyn in her arms as the last of his life force left him.

He seemed so much smaller without the power of the Mark behind him. As light as a child.

Ivloch lay motionless among the dead.

There was no one to hear the cries Becca Jenns unleashed into the night.

Eighteen

It could have been hours, but it felt like days by the time he awoke.

He had relived every part of his short but messy life. Ma's beaming face felt like it had never gone away. Kreg's delight at marrying Esmerelda on his blessing day. Even fond memories of Lusha taking him on his first fishing trip.

It was only Becca's face there as he shifted himself up; tear-streaked and ashen.

He didn't know how she had dug a hole or managed to carry Edwyn to it, but she had. He was wrapped in the remains of Ivloch's cloak, the fabric cocooning his cold, frail body.

"He was scared at the end, you could tell, but he tried to be brave." She clung to the fabric of Ivloch's tunic and wept. The arrow had been ripped from her arm, but she had done little to patch the wound.

He felt his wrist throb as it tucked around Becca's waist. He moved it gingerly, afraid of what he would see.

The Mark was there. As dark and bold as it had been on Edwyn Jenns.

He felt different. As if someone had injected him with adrenaline that refused to wane, his muscles tighter, his brain running in too many directions, yet somehow more focused than ever.

Is this what the Mark did to a person? If deemed worthy? Could it then enhance the bearer? Or was it just an after effect from the memories he had been forced to relive?

"They will be coming, Ivloch. We must prepare you."

"I think…it's telling me certain things. About how Kara's Guild began, about your vows. I didn't know them before but now they're in my head. Greetings, positions. It's…odd."

It was. He could recite The Guild vow if she asked him to. Conduct the ceremony even. He was certain he could walk to the Black Lands without a guide. The image of a Darkstar was there; yet he had never even seen a picture, only vague descriptions.

Then there was another thing. A box his mind wanted him to wait to open. A warning about the demon Edwyn had described. Later. He would face it when he had the time; the ability to comprehend what the secret entailed. When Becca wasn't there to see his reaction. If it had been something Edwyn couldn't handle; then he doubted Becca would not notice his pain.

"I…Edwyn received information when he was a child. He knew it as he grew up. Perhaps it is different if you're not born with it?" Becca seemed confused, studying him as if he was a riddle she had to solve.

"It is. Knowledge must be passed. A child must learn; a risk we are forced to take. One who passes the test must know what is to come immediately. It is the only way we can prepare." He surprised himself with the words and Becca stepped back.

"Ivloch…oh Kara, I'm sorry."

"She did this, Bec." He was aware it was the first time he had called her Bec and gasped. "Kara wanted this for her Guardians. It's…not a bad thing."

"But not a good one?"

"We have to let time tell that, don't we? There's a lot we need to ruddy do with it."

"…And never enough of it."

He pulled her towards him as he became distantly aware of the flap of wings. Wings which flew from the south.

Eshaa had brought the help she promised or the Mark passing to him would not matter. He doubted it could protect him from a hungry Darkstar.

"They're here, Becca. Any moment."

She knelt before him, her hands entwined in his. "Then may I be the first to swear my fealty to the new leader of Kara's Guild. I serve you for the sake of Brodanna, this moon and all those to follow, Ivloch Youchnore." She smiled but he could see the hesitation in her eyes. The dread for what those moons would contain.

"You serve beside me and only there, Becca. Always." She would, for as long as time would allow it. It was her brother's dream and her people and he would be damned if he wouldn't do all he could to save them for her. "Jefferson is going to be terrible, The Unforgiven even more so, but we do this together."

She was standing proudly next to him as the Darkstars descended on the field below them.

Three of the beasts. Black or golden scales along most of their bodies and the curve of their wings. Teeth thicker than his arm. Red armour across their flanks and bellies. Four legs each, lower limbs which were bigger than any dwelling or inn he had ever visited and a tail which swung out behind them to end in a deadly shaped tip.

Esmerelda had once compared them to the dragons of Earth's old stories, but he hadn't believed her. The similarities of those giant heads, each one such a different vibrant colour, made him realise he owed her quite the apology.

A lot had happened to Ivloch Youchnore in the past three moon turns, but this felt the most inexplicable.

One leaned to the side and unleashed a snapping clap towards an upturned bush. It disappeared under the might of its ferocious claws in seconds. A threatening tongue slid from its mouth before it reared back. Flames rained down on the spot the growth had been. A roar, so mighty, unleashed from the green-headed Darkstar next to it.

"I…" words were failing him.

"Wait until one asks you to pet it," Becca laughed. Despite everything she could still see the hidden joy in the world. It amazed him. It was a sound he didn't think he would ever get sick of hearing.

Riders slid from their backs as the Darkstars stomped across the green. The world suddenly seemed a little smaller.

Eshaa ran at the front of them, her hair windswept, but her furs still perfectly in place. Behind her trailed three women and two men. All with the kohl across their eyes and covered in nearly as much rough fur as she.

"Edwyn?" She wasted no time, as he had expected.

"Edwyn has passed." Becca's softness was gone, The Guild member standing in her place.

"The Mark?" The question came from a large woman behind her. Her furs only reached her elbows and Ivloch could see a Mark, the same one he now carried, on her right wrist, a diamond in place of the circle.

She shielded a girl behind her, but the girl seemed determined to poke her head out and stare at him and Becca. She was his own age, her short cropped white hair, stark against the stormy sky behind her.

"The Mark now belongs to Ivloch Youchnore, the new leader of Kara's Guild. I have already sworn my allegiance and I suggest you do the same," Becca declared. He vaguely listened to her continue on about how Edwyn had been training him in secret, he was a formidable warrior. The lies that he hated but knew were necessary. From both Edwyn and the knowledge now inside him.

One of the men appeared at a bewildered Eshaa's side, an axe in hand. She could be the undoing of it all. "These dead King's Men. Who killed them?"

"I did." Ivloch knew this was his chance. "They attacked our camp to their folly, and I dispatched them as was needed. I will always do what is necessary to protect you and the people of Brodanna."

Becca squeezed his hand lightly. If he was impressing her then that was half the battle.

The man and other Guardian exchanged a look and Ivloch tried not to think of what those Darkstars could do if they ordered them to… The girl pushed past her carer and only stopped when she reached him.

His Mark throbbed in anticipation and he knew exactly who she was.

She bowed before him and raised her own wrist. It was so like his, but with a K and not the G.

"I'm Dorlya of the Black Lands, Kara's Marked. I welcome you, Guild Leader. Protect me as you see fit and honour those who believe in our ways."

Ivloch knew he should also kneel; his legs began the movement before he even asked them to.

"I, Ivloch Youchnore, thank you, Dorlya, for your acceptance and promise to serve you and your line for all my moons."

Their Marks called to one another as their hands bound together. "For Brodanna," they whispered in unison.

If Kara's Marked accepted him then the Black Lands would not be able to disobey. It was the way of it and the new power told him so. Edwyn's separation and dreams could continue. There might be a chance to save the people of Brodanna; to stop The Unforgiven.

The other four all knelt to recite the words Becca had insisted on saying first.

Ivloch Youchnore had their vows and their allegiance.

Eshaa said nothing as Dorlya and the Guardian she introduced him to, Jenn, led them towards the Darkstars. Ivloch did everything in his power not to flinch as the mighty creature looked down at him and seemed to consider him not worthy of a fight.

"You ride with me," Eshaa demanded. Ivloch and Becca followed her towards the sandy coloured Darkstar on the right. "You lied to them," she continued.

"We did what we had to. Will you tell them?" Becca had clearly decided preamble or excuses weren't a necessity for Eshaa's sensibilities.

Her Darkstar let her touch his outstretched wing, as she seemed to consider Becca's query. Ivloch couldn't help but focus on the way the scales caught the sun or how the wings were as long as the tallest tree on Brodanna. To live a life without seeing such a thing would have been heart-breaking.

"I will keep silent, for Edwyn and what comes next, but one day you will owe me, Ivloch Youchnore, and I will call in such a debt." Eshaa glared at him and there was little to do but nod in agreement. A pact he hoped he would not come to regret. Becca seemed uncertain; but she had a practical mind. There was no other choice available for The Guild.

"Now we ride." The wing folded to create steps on which they could mount. Eshaa went first, laughing at Ivloch's utter reluctance, as Becca followed silently.

He had been an apprentice in Rightwy and now he was the leader of Kara's Guild and about to fly on a Darkstar.

If Ma could see him now…

"To the Black Lands Commander…" Eshaa screamed as she patted the beast's neck and they began to ascend into the clouds.

TWENTY-THREE YEARS LATER.
IN THE SEASON OF AWAKENING.

DURING THE EVENTS OF THE CAGED KINGDOM.

Ivloch

He remembered the first time he had ever seen The Black City, built in to the mountain, as he approached again. Riding on the back of a Darkstar, with Becca at his side, was certainly different to approaching alone and unarmed.

Too much had changed; with too few answers along the way. The last few years had not always been kind to him; but the next would be worse. Part of the secret he had carried for so long, coming to fruition. A shard of truth he had never whispered, to anyone, but had weighted every one of his moons.

The signs were here.

He had not decoded the puzzle, or found more pieces than his own, but the ancient magic in his veins still warned him that change was nigh. The reason he had been forced to revisit the Black Lands; to beg and plead for any help they could provide.

He had ruined their alliance to protect The Guild; but had deep down, always known this day was coming.

A war could not be won alone, by anyone.

The mountain stretched up and across as far as his eyes could see, dwellings built into the rocks on every level. Two Darkstars flew freely along the boundary but seemed to pay him and Yemtree, his mount, no attention.

Twenty years since he had seen anyone inside.

Riding south had given him too many memories; the worst time to remember how he and Becca had begun.

The temptation to turn back had been strong but he was here for a reason. Kara's Guild and everything they had worked so hard to accomplish was at risk. The war they had feared for so long was about to begin. Ivloch had been the only man that could make this trek and stand a chance of success.

If Edwyn had never given up, then neither would he.

There was only one gate into the Black Lands and a man-made ridge was carved into the mountain above it. One that was heavily guarded by their finest soldiers, and oh, he knew they made them well here. He would be dead before he had a chance to call Becca's name, if they wished it so.

Only the Mark had given him no warning... A small comfort, but one he had no choice, but to ferociously cling to.

They would be able to see him from this distance. Weapons would be aimed at his head and heart. The Dark Council would have been summoned to the battlements; their ruling would be as final as it always was.

He could only hope Eshaa had kept her promise to end up on that council or his life would be forfeit. The lives of the people he cared about, who hadn't already fallen, at even more risk. He had lost too many lost along the way. If there was another life, he hoped Esmerelda and Kreg knew he had kept his promise to care for their child. How strong that woman had become. How much he loved her.

He raised his hands as he reached the gate, acutely aware of the bow strings pulled tight.

"Who dares attempt to enter the Black Lands?" It was more of a demand than a question.

"Ivloch Youchnore. Leader of Kara's Guild and former friend, and ally, too many of you."

The silence felt like it would never end.

He was greyer than he had been on any other visit. Wiser, Older. Horribly more open to compromise.

They had once vowed to defeat The Unforgiven together, for the sake of Brodanna, a vow once so sacred, ruined by petty politics and the simple tempers of man.

The Unforgiven were here and waiting for them both. Hidden in their people, taking the ones they had sworn to protect. Jefferson had succeeded in creating the hole in the barrier. There was no longer time to hold grudges or pretend they didn't need one another.

The giant gates creaked open just as he thought they never would. To return empty handed would have been worst of all.

They opened to a courtyard which reached into the sky. All who lived up the mountain would be able to see his entrance. Fur covered guards created a walkway which he urged a nervous Yemtree to follow.

The face that came to meet him halfway was a familiar one. One he hadn't seen since Dorlya's death, when The Guild rode north, never to return.

"Hello old friend. We've been expecting you. I guess you want to repay that debt after all?"

Eshaa had aged, much like he had, but she was as formidable as ever. The slightest grey dotted her scalp and her body had filled out over the years. He tried to pay no attention to the other soldiers surrounding her or the legions of Black Landers wandering freely into the distance; going about their daily business.

"I'm here to discuss terms, Eshaa. I'll do as you ask if you help me first." She had asked him to do something before he travelled north. Ivloch had refused; but there was no longer time for such weaknesses of the heart.

"Always was a condition with you, Youchnore. Come. Let's discuss it with the Dark Council. Perhaps we will find a resolution to suit us all. Zecane, take the horse."

Eshaa shook his hand briskly and began to walk. She knew he would follow, as Yemtree's reigns were taken by a warrior from her guard. More kohl on his eyes than Ivloch expected from Katanya, his shoulder length hair dyed half blue and half black.

"I'll care for your mount well, Guild leader," he remarked as Yemtree licked his out stretched hand.

Ivloch tilted his hands in a semblance of thanks. It would take time to adjust to how these people handled themselves again. A skill he had previously been so adept at, much to Becca's surprise.

"We heard about your wife," Eshaa announced as they paced. He let no surprise show. Despite their solitude, the Black Lands had obviously kept up their information network.

"I take it you made the Council?"

"I told you I would, so I did. Did you expect anything less, Youchnore? We will drive a hard bargain."

He knew; had always known. It didn't matter anymore; he would do whatever needed to be done to save Brodanna. Even if that meant agreeing to terms which would be very hard to live with.

"Then we should hope I learnt to negotiate in our time apart."

The ruthless grin she first displayed in the woods, so long ago, crept across her striking face once more.

There was only one phrase which remained in his mind, as Eshaa ushered him into the hollowed-out mountain.

Fools and Heroes.

Fools and Heroes both end up dead in the end.

Only history would decide which one he was.

A history he had to make sure occurred.

Ivloch will return in:

The Caged Kingdom

Book One of The Unforgiven Series

Currently available for purchase on all Amazon Marketplaces.

Please turn the page to read the first chapter...

The sequel:

The Heir to Chaos

is coming July 2019.

Extract from the Book of the Lands - published on the Moon Cycle of the creation of Brodanna by High Priestess Adyra George.
Inscription can also be found on the tomb of Queen Kara of the Blessed Blood, located in Tonkara.

.

We lived on Earth as one.
It was The Curse that caused us to leave.
A sickness that swept the world; to reveal those with an unknown,
only guessed upon gift.
We could wield fire, we could heal, and we could move things with
our minds.
Some said we were stronger, better. Some said we were evil, an
abomination hidden in their ranks.
Some said we were as old a tale as time itself.
They said it was magic; they proclaimed us a danger.
We did not want to burn like our ancestors, so we fled.
We left and we flourished.
Seven worlds to grow on, our power unleashed, infinite as we could
be.
We created utopia.
Generations of power, diplomacy, and wonder.
Then we turned on each other; planets burned, and we died.
We will not wipe out those responsible; we are better than that,
better than them…
But they will not live among us.
They will be cursed forever more, sent away to seal their own fates.
All who wish to travel with them may.
To strive or perish will be their choice.
They will be the people of Brodanna.

One – Elex

Death had walked beside her since she could lift a blade. It came to her as a friend, in the bleak of the night or when the sun was highest in the sky. It always felt like coming home. She was its weapon, its glory, and its fuel. The only constant companion she had ever known.

Tonight, it would also be her last.

The Facility where she had been undercover for half a year, six whole moon turns, raged above her. Wielders who worked for the King, fighting the men and women she had spent her life beside. Scared prisoners, taken for their power, running whilst they had the chance. A fleeting possibility of escape better than a life of misery as a slave.

She had always known this battle would take place. Her time here, her own idea. Kara's Guild had reluctantly accepted the plan.

War had been brewing on Brodanna for a very long time and anything that gave them a chance to protect its people was a risk worth taking.

The people she loved would be above, searching for her and their objective, an artefact of great power The Guild was sworn to protect. Somewhere in this fortress was the sword of the martyred Queen Kara. The very same Kara who had given her life to cast the spell which would keep their world safe from the predations of The Unforgiven. The incantation that had made Elex Carter's existence a misery.

The relic had been in the hands of their enemy for too long. If rumours were true, they also possessed one of the Guardians, held in a matching Facility outside Torlung. If they found the others, if they had known of the Mark that had, until recently, adorned her flesh... She shuddered at the thought...

It would have meant the plan brought her enemy another step closer to escaping and having the power to lower the barrier that protected their world. The previous attempt had been why Kara was forced to pay such a price. A cost that had only passed to Elex. It had been a dangerous game, but one she needed to play.

Navigating the winding building had been easier than she predicted. The King's Men and Users were preoccupied with the incoming attack, shouts of anger or bewilderment that The Guild had passed their defences coming from every direction. Her power, so diminished compared to what it had been, still rallied to her aid.

Every door that remained locked had sprung open at her touch. Elex had made her way through four levels, pausing only to assist any still-detained captives.

She knew where she had to go. Where this entire plan had really been leading her all along. Prince Hamill Landress would be on the basement level with his devoted guards.

The eldest of the King's children had been one of the first The Unforgiven claimed. The man he was before, gone.

He would never normally have set foot in such a place. It was, after all, a glorified supply store. One that the detainees here were forced to work in. Labour which had to occur, regardless of any injuries suffered at the hands of the Facilities' guards or the Users they forced to do their bidding. Even when the test drugs ran through their systems or after moons of torture. There was no escape, no help, no reprieve. Her fists tightened at the memories of the cruelty she had been forced to see.

The atrocities which had been allowed to occur across Brodanna all in King Jefferson's name.

A guard leaped out at her as she neared the stairs which would take her to the Prince. She reached for a weapon she didn't have. An old habit. One she would never perform again.

He came at her with an axe, bringing it down in a blow intended for her head, but she swung her body to the left and dodged the assault. He roared and advanced again.

She gave him no chance to touch her as she summoned her favourite party trick. Whirls of dark steel formed in her hands. They were darting for his neck before he had time to lift the axe again. His body fell at her feet as her blades dissolved from existence.

"May The Transmitter rest your soul," she cooed, stepping over the corpse.

Time was running out. The fighting would be getting closer. Ivloch and Camrin would have realised she had lied to them by now. They may have even found Mara. She hoped they had found the girl. If Xave got to her first…

Elex reached for the handle and pulled. It didn't budge. Another will of the heat inside her. It flew open, nearly knocking her from her feet. The harsh light gave her a headache as she started to descend the perfectly white staircase.

Every journey must reach an end.

***

The Transmitter had taken her ancestors from Earth. A journey she couldn't imagine. Whoever he or they were had provided for the people. Ships which carried thousands away from a hatred that had swept their home. New planets provided for them to live on.

If only there had been a thought to remove their humanity whilst they were there.

The Seven Worlds had not been enough. The law and order of magic didn't provide some with enough power, so they wished to rewrite it. If magic was what their gifts really were. Some called it an evolution, others a fluke. The M word had simply been an outdated idea which stuck. She could understand why some hated it but it didn't bother her. She was who she was. A label would not change that. It never had.

Brodanna came after the war. A cage for the criminals who had caused so much destruction, all for their own gain. A place her ancestors had decided to go, like so many did. She hated them.

If they hadn't made such an awful decision, this destiny would never have been hers. She could have lived to a ripe old age with a pretty garden and Camrin by her side.

The notion made her laugh as she reached the final step. An equally luminous corridor stretched before her. Life would have never worked out that way and The Transmitter had abandoned her.

She refused to let herself think of Camrin, instead she focused on moving forward. Her bare feet freezing on the white stone floor. Katanya, the only person who had known she had changed the plan, would be horrified if she knew her sister was to die without a good set of boots on her feet. Kat wouldn't be above; she was no longer with The Guild and had refused to ever take their holy vow. It would have been nice to see her one last time.

Katanya would only do her bit once Elex was gone.

She would also be enraged when she discovered Elex had deceived her, but Elex was owed a debt, an obligation she had called in to get the help she needed.

Kat had been the only logical half-accomplice. Despite the dishonesty, she would do what she must. That was what mattered.

Even if none of them would ever know why.

There were three rooms here. She had to move quickly or everything she wanted to achieve would fail. Worse, her friends might find her. All her lies uncovered and a future she could not face. Would not face.

Her feet glided forward, the chill spreading through the red overalls she was forced to wear. She reached up and pulled the matching twine from her blonde hair letting it fall around her shoulders and over the arch of her back. She loved her hair. The feel of it, the things she could do with it, the way Camrin sniffed it... It should be free for what was to come.

She caught sight of her naked wrist as she lowered her arm. It looked so empty without the Mark that she had been born with. The matching one which had scrolled across her abdomen would also be gone. She had used her abilities to hide them whilst stuck here and adjusted, to an extent, to the sight of them missing. She knew this time they would not be coming back. Their power and meaning rested with someone else now.

She was no longer Marked by Kara. The Guild had no obligation to protect her anymore. The blood of Brodanna's queen no longer etched itself in her veins. She would die a simple Wielder.

Mara Lars was hopefully upstairs being rescued. Ivloch would find the Marks on the young woman and understand. He was one of the few left in Brodanna who knew the entire truth of The Unforgiven and Kara's sacrifice. He would also know Elex had known this was coming, hopefully her note would help him understand her choice.

Kara's chosen and the five Guardians who were sworn to protect her had an inherent alarm system built into their Marks. A day's warning that their death was imminent; whether that be by natural causes, their own choice or an enemy's blade. They could pass their Mark on in that time if they knew a worthy recipient, as she herself had done, or they could die with it belonging to them. Kara's spell would search the land and discover who was ready to take the mantle.

A system that would never end until The Unforgiven were vanquished, not just concealed, so Brodanna may have a chance to flourish. Kara's only option meant their return one day, a future generation destined to fight them. Little had she known that Users would become rarer and rarer under the barrier that protected them, or that a ruthless king, an ill-deserving descendent of her bloodline would help them achieve such a thing. If only that time hadn't been Elex's.

She had reached the first room to her left. It was empty. The usual uniforms stacked high, User-resistant handcuffs scattered across the desk, weapons along the wall. She considered taking one but decided against it. Her power may be diminished but she did not expect it to fail her or the legacy she would leave behind.

A legacy which should have been better. She was never going to be the ideal face of a rebellion. Too prone to half-truths and letting those she loved down. But there were so many things she could have done...

Another empty room to the right contained nothing but food rations and files. Hamill would be in the last room, mere metres away. Her brain kept calling him Hamill, but she knew he wasn't the King's son anymore.

She would never understand how the King had offered up his first-born as a host, a prized gift to form an alliance of hatred that would spiral the world into war.

A war she would no longer be a part of.

Neither would Hamill Landress.

He would be stronger and more powerful than her, of that she was certain. There had never been an intention to walk away from this fight. The only hope was that she would be able to take him with her. One last gift to The Guild.

His visit here had been planned as long as her time in the Facility. The final card to fall into place. She hadn't told Ivloch. He was hers to take, the thing that she needed.

Elex had never planned to leave the Tonkara Facility alive, but she sure as hell wanted to go out on her own terms.

She moved to the door of the third room, willing her power to be ready. One last dance, together.

She had discovered she was dying a year ago. There were pains that wouldn't leave. A visit to an Unpowered healer in Wylow, one she knew could be trusted, had confirmed her fears. Power could accomplish many things, but it could rarely heal the flesh. There had been nothing anyone could do.

The Guild didn't know. Camrin didn't know.

She was their hope. How could they see a future where the one vow they put above all else could not be held? They could not protect her from nature's intentions.

She had learnt to hold a blade as soon as she was able to wield her power like one. If she had to die, then she would die with it in her hands. The dark steel formed as it had before. They would do her bidding and not fail her.

She was Elex Carter, the ferocious former holder of Kara's Mark and to hell with anyone who ever said different.

She kicked open the door…

Death was to be her first and final friend.

The Caged Kingdom

Available on Amazon now.

Thank you so much for reading Ivloch!

I hope you enjoyed Ivloch's story and it would mean the world to me if you could leave a review on Amazon or Goodreads.

Reviews will help new readers discover the world of Brodanna and they help Authors like me keep doing what we.

I very much hope you will read The Caged Kingdom and continue your Unforgiven Series adventure.

If you want to discover more about The Unforgiven Series or gain access to other exclusive novellas please sign up to my newsletter at www.mapricewriting.com.

I'd also love to hear from you on social media:

Twitter: @MAPriceAuthor
Instagram: @M.A.PriceAuthor
Facebook: @M.A.PriceAuthor

Acknowledgements

A massive thank you to everyone who has read this book. You are the most important thing. I know how long reading a book takes and how many wonderful ones are out there. Your time, thoughts and support is appreciated more than I can say.

I'm a little amazed I'm writing my second set of acknowledgements. It's not something I ever thought I'd do once, let alone twice. I am definitely not complaining though, especially if you've stuck around to read them.

I'd like to thank my husband Brad. He loved this story and the characters in it, particularly Edwyn. It really helped me fall in love with an earlier version of Brodanna and was an absolute joy to see.

To my friends again: I wouldn't be me without you. You complete me and make me so amazingly happy. Your love and support for this book and The Caged Kingdom has made me cry and feel incredibly lucky.

I'd like to give a special shout out to: Scarlet, Lauren, Cheyenne and all my other favourite ladies. You're all so talented, beautiful and passionate; thank you for being the best girl gang.

A big thanks to Mike for coping with all the book chats and I hope you avoided most of the spoilers! I promise we will find some hungover Sundays just to watch trashy films again, in all their awful glory.

I want to go on and list you all now, but I shouldn't. I do love you though and I'll make sure I thank you all in person/the next book.

An extra thanks to Mark Skinner for the wonderful cover again. If you're a Dungeons and Dragons fan then I highly recommend you check out his Magic Maps page. It's incredible.

Heather Titus also deserves a mention for being a wonderful and easy editor to work with! You're a star.
Ivloch Youchnore has been a character milling around in my head for years. His bushy beard has always been desperate to reach the pages of a book and I'm so glad he convinced me he needed his own novella.

It's just a small taste of Brodanna, but it's a wonderful one. I hope you'll come along on the rest of the journey.

About The Author

M. A. Price lives in Cambridge, England with her husband and army of slightly podgy cats. She's a massive sci-fi and fantasy nerd and can usually be found watching Star Trek or reading. She has previously worked in freelance journalism but moved towards finally brining the stories from her head to life in 2018. The Unforgiven Series is her first fantasy instalment, with many more to come.